THE SISTER WIFE'S SEARCH

A GRAY WEST MYSTERY BOOK 2

ANYA MORA

Printed in the United States of America

THE SISTER WIFE'S SEARCH

A GRAY WEST MYSTERY BOOK 2

By Anya Mora

I'm more than a single mom running from the cult that held me captive—I'm a woman carving out a life for myself.

It's harder than I expected.

After solving the murder of my best friend, I'm hoping my run-ins with the law are over.

Then my eight-year-old daughter goes missing.

Local detective, and friend, Boone, is on the case, and the neighborhood is determined to help find my little girl alive.

But the clock is ticking. And hope? It's running out.

A kidnapped child is a mother's worst nightmare.

I will search until she is found, even if it means confronting my past. My sister wives might have the clue I need, and I'm no longer scared of them.

I'm a mother on a mission, and losing Ruthie isn't an option.

1

HE'S TALLER than I remembered. Taller than me now.

"Abel." My voice is a near whisper as I pull my son into a hug, breathing him in, scared that he will leave before I've got a chance to let him know just how sorry I am.

A year ago, I left Garden Temple without telling him, my sister wives, or my husband where I was going.

I didn't trust any of them enough to let me leave without a fight.

So I took my daughters and fled.

But that decision meant leaving behind my fifteen-year-old son, a young man who looks more like his father than I remembered. He's grown so much in the last year.

Abel's eyes are rimmed in red, and I wonder how he even got here. A bus probably, with stolen money.

"You've been coming here, other times?" I ask, thinking of the glass Coke bottle on the counter, seeing a shadowy figure running from the back steps.

"A few times," he says, nodding. "But I kept second-guessing myself. Didn't know if Dad was right, if Garden Temple is the righteous way. I've been torn, Mom." He runs a hand through his light hair.

"Why did you make yourself known now?" I ask, looking down the dark street. Olive and Ruthie are at Luna's house. I need to get them. The temperature is dropping, and it feels like the snow that was predicted might actually fall.

I'm still reeling from the day I've had. Elle's confession to murder. Me, lifting the plaque, slamming it down over her head. Her body unconscious, her blood spilled on the tiled floor. The police coming, taking reports. Boone's eyes on mine. "Can I call you?" he'd asked. I'd told him no. That I would reach out when there was a good time.

Now Abel is here, the past at my doorstep, and I am glad I told Boone no.

The timing isn't right. I doubt it ever will be.

"I need your help, Mom," Abel repeats.

"Is it about Bethany?" I ask, my voice soft, scared to say or do anything that might have him retreating once more. The last thing I want is to see my son running after he just came back to me.

His shoulders fall, and my heart falls too. Bethany was his childhood best friend; they loved one another in their own ways. And I know, too, that losing the girl he cared so deeply for, to his father, is a pill too bitter to swallow.

"You knew, then? That Dad's gonna marry her?"

"Lydia told me," I confess.

"You've talked to her?" He furrows his eyebrows.

"A few times. I was worried your dad was looking for me."

Abel scoffs. "He wasn't. He was too busy with Bethany. The ceremony is set for the end of the week."

I press my fingers to my temples, trying to focus. Tired is the tip of the iceberg. I've been running on fumes all week.

"We'll figure this out, I promise," I tell

him, having no idea how to make good on my word. I pull my son into my arms. Holding him tight. Not wanting to let go. He's here now, and I'll fight to keep it that way.

An hour later, I'm trying to stay alert after a long day. Police reports, an ambulance, blood on the floor. Piecing together the deaths of my friends. It has worn me out in ways I haven't begun to process.

With a pizza box on the table, everyone digs in. Thankfully, Luna, the neighbor, didn't press me for details about anything. She seemed to sense I was too tired to talk, to explain. She will see it all in the news soon enough.

Now I sit at the kitchen table with Olive, Ruthie, and Abel. My three children, here with me.

Olive can't stop touching Abel's arm. "I can believe you're really here."

Ruthie asks if this means she has to move into Olive's room so Abel can have hers.

"I don't know, sweetie," I tell her honestly. I want to say more, but the truth is I don't know Abel's intentions.

Tears keep falling down my cheeks, and Abel doesn't understand why I'm so weepy.

"It's not just seeing you that's making her cry," Olive, the brightest twelve-year-old I know, explains to her big brother. "It's been a crazy few weeks. Her friend was murdered."

Abel's eyes widen. "Seriously?"

Ruthie picks the mushrooms off her pizza slice. "Yeah, he was a liar, Abel." At eight, she doesn't understand tact. "But so is Dad, so maybe all guys are?" She looks her brother directly in the eyes. "Are you?"

Olive snaps, "Ruthie, are you stupid?"

Ruthie's face falls, and she turns to me with crocodile tears. The sisters might bicker and tease, but they never jump at one another like that.

"Olive, apologize," I say softly.

Olive groans. "Me? Why? She's the one asking dumb questions."

"I'm not stupid!" Ruthie pushes back.

Olive rolls her eyes dramatically. "I didn't say you were, just that the question was. God!"

That word gets Abel's attention. "What's happened to you all? Speaking like this, and you didn't even say grace before dinner."

Olive and Ruthie's eyes meet. And with

that, at least, they've found common ground. "We don't believe in things that they teach at Garden Temple anymore," Olive says. "It's why we left."

"Didn't you leave because Mom tricked you?" Abel asks, trying to see where their alliances lie. But we don't play manipulative games at this house like he's used to.

"Dad wanted me to get married in, like, a year," Olive says, her back now straight, confident in her reasoning. "Which is bonkers. I'm in seventh grade."

Abel runs a hand over his jaw, then rests his elbows on the table as if exhausted. "Yeah, that's why I'm here. Dad's taking a new wife."

"Who?" Olive asks.

In the past, my instinct would have been to rein in this conversation, to protect their father. But that was the old me. That was Grace, bound to Jeremiah, sister wife to Naomi and Lydia, believer in the prophet, daughter of God.

Now I am Gray West, a single mom who is done with secrets, done living a life of lies. I won't stop my children from talking about the truth, even if it's painful. Even if it means the people we used to be no longer exist.

"Dad is marrying Bethany," Abel says, the

room becoming so quiet, so still, at the name. Everyone at the table knows that Abel and Bethany were two peas in a pod since they could walk, best friends until it was deemed inappropriate for a teen boy to be so close with a sister-in-Christ. Still, they found ways to stay close, and I never said a word about it to Jeremiah. But he is the prophet, so he knew. Knows. He chose Bethany to be his next wife to send a message.

His son has heard it, loud and clear. *I am in complete control.*

"Bethany?" Ruthie frowns, trying to connect the dots. "Your Bethany?"

Abel's eyes have turned dark, but not menacing. Broken. "Yeah, Ruthie. That Bethany."

"But..." Ruthie shakes her head, clearly confused. In her eyes, Bethany was the sweet friend of her big brother, the girl who sang like a songbird at services, the girl with auburn hair and pale-blue eyes.

Olive wipes at the tears falling down her cheeks. "Dad wouldn't." Disbelief in her voice, fear in eyes.

"The wedding is in six days," Abel continues. "It's why I finally came here. For help. I need your help, Mom."

“What do you want me to do?” I ask. “You know your father.”

“I want you to tell him not to do this to me. I love her, Mom. I love Bethany.”

Tears fill my eyes now too. “You always have.”

“Please,” he begs. “Make him change his mind.”

Olive sits up straight. “You can’t change Dad’s mind. He’s infallible.”

“Big word for a girl,” Abel says.

Olive smirks. “Yeah, in the real world, girls go to school just like boys.”

“Yeah?” Abel asks. “You do realize the cost of all that equality, don’t you?”

Olive frowns, clearly unsure of what to think of her brother. “Why did you come here if you still love the compound so much?”

It’s the question I’ve wanted to ask, and I’m glad she spoke up. Her using her voice is the reason I was so intent on getting my daughters away from Garden Temple. I wanted my girls to think on their own. And they are.

The cost, though, means their brother is on the outs, and their father is not in their lives.

“Bethany doesn’t want to marry Dad,”

Abel explains. "That's why I came here. For help. But it's hard to see how brainwashed Mom has let you become."

Olive groans. "You don't know anything about us."

"I know this family is in ruins." Abel's voice is hard as he looks at me. "If you hadn't left, he would never have gone after Bethany."

"You're blaming me now?" I ask, running my hands over my face, exhausted.

"Don't fight," Ruthie says, and the simple request from the youngest person in the room gets my attention. "Please."

I need to take control of the situation. "Look, it's been a very long day, and I am exhausted. I'm happy you're here, Abel. I am. But we can't figure this all out tonight."

"Tomorrow?" he presses.

"Of course," I say, reaching out and squeezing his hand. "After I get off work and your sisters are home from school; we'll make a plan, okay?"

"We don't have school," Ruthie says. "It's called an in-service day."

Olive nods. "She's right. We have a three-day weekend."

"Well, we'll deal with that tomorrow. Right now, you both need showers."

By the time I get the girls in bed, and the couch made up for Abel, my whole body threatens to give out. I need sleep.

Still, I sit on the couch next to my oldest child and rest a hand on his back. Is a mother's work ever done?

"I'm so happy to have you here," I tell him. "And I know dinner got tense, but listen, we've had a long week here, and we need to recover."

"I get it," he says. "It's insane—a murder?"

I nod. Patrick gone, Anna too. My business folded. My new friendship with Boone —the last person I should be close with. He is a detective. Looking for clues is his job, and I don't want any of my secrets coming out beyond the four walls of this house.

"How did you know where to find us?" I ask. It's the question that I need answered, and I'm scared of what he is going to say.

"It's not what you think," he admits. "Dad doesn't know where you are; at least he's never mentioned it."

"I spoke with Lydia, but never told her where we are. So how did you know?"

Abel drops his head back. "You won't like

to hear this, but Olive sent me a letter. Luckily I saw it before anyone else. It was the week after you left."

"Olive?" I can't be upset; she's a child, torn from the only family she has ever known. Of course she reached out to Abel. A year ago, she was so angry I made her leave. "Did you tell anyone you were coming?"

Abel's jaw twitches. "Bethany knew. She's scared, Mom. Really scared."

I press my lips together, needing more time to think this through. "Your father won't let Bethany leave freely, and even if he did, he wouldn't let you be with her," I say. "What do you want to happen?"

Abel drops his head in his hands. "I want to be with her."

"That means the both of you leaving Garden Temple, for good."

Abel nods. "I don't know if she'll agree. She has never left the compound in her entire life. I never had either, except to go to the build site."

"Are they still working on that?" The build site is where the men of Garden Temple are constructing our paradise. Eventually the women will be allowed, but not until it is complete. Now I wonder what they're really doing. I'll ask Abel, now that there are cracks in his alliance with his father, but tonight isn't the time.

"Yeah, and sometimes we'd stop at the Handy's Pit Stop for food or whatever. I know it's wrong, but I stole money from Dad for bus fare. I got more comfortable with the idea of leaving. Of sneaking away at night on a bus. Of coming here."

"It's a long trip," I say, thinking of the five-hour trek from the compound to Tacoma. "No one ever noticed you were gone?"

Abel smirks. "I think Dad has had enough on his plate, and without a mom around to keep me in check, I was free more than I should have been. And I only came here twice."

"Twice?" I ask, remembering all the times over the last few weeks I thought someone had broken in, realizing each incident wasn't Abel, but probably the drug dealers that were looking for Patrick's inventory in my garage.

"Yeah, and I wasn't planning on coming today, but then Dad announced the ceremony was next week and I panicked. I ran."

"I'm sorry I left without you," I say. "I thought if I told you, you would—"

My son cuts me off. "I get it, you don't

have to explain. I know it's strange, but I came here a few times, and watched you and the girls. And you are different here than you were at the compound."

"Different, how?" I ask, wanting to believe him. Wanting to believe I am more than I was. A broken woman, walking on eggshells, the sum of my life full of cracks. I want to be someone my children can be proud of. Someone I can be proud of.

"You seem stronger now. Like you're not afraid to fight."

My voice catches in my throat. "I wish things had been different. That you could have come."

He shakes his head. "No. I had to stay. For Bethany. She needs me now."

I smile somehow. "I think you're stronger now too. Less afraid."

Abel, my son who is so nearly a man, smiles too. "In that case, I guess Dad won't see our strength coming."

My heart falls. Abel doesn't understand he is asking the impossible of me.

Abel is so naïve. Strength won't help when it comes to his father.

2

I WAKE up to texts from the neighbor ladies. They've put me in a group chat, which should be a benchmark to integrating as a normal suburban mom, but I feel like I'll be exposed as a fraud at any moment.

KENDALL: *OMG just read the* Tacoma Tribune*. They found your friend's killer?! Are you okay, Gray?*

Julia: *Just caught up. Gray—I saw in a FB group that you were there? They have a photo of you w/the cops outside a house?*

. . .

Reading it causes my heart to race. A photo of me on the internet?

Luna: ***I saw that too. I can screenshot for you, I know you're not on social media, Gray.***

A moment later, the photo comes through. It's not so bad—and you would have to know who I was to even think it was me.

The clickbait caption reads, "Local woman fends off killer."

No name. Thank goodness.

Me: ***It was all so horrific. Grateful to have the case closed—I've been a wreck.***

Julia: ***Let us know how we can help. I hear there is gonna be snow this weekend. Maybe we can go sledding with the kids? Hot toddies for the mamas?!? Who's in?***

And just like that, the women are preparing to move on. Snow days and spiked drinks, and pretending that two murders didn't just happen. I shove my phone in my back jeans pocket, not emotionally prepared to engage any further with the neighbors.

I hear the girls getting up, smell coffee brewing. That makes me smile. Abel started drinking coffee when he turned thirteen, a habit I let slide because, being one of his three mothers, it wasn't often I got to give him what he wanted. Walking down the hall, Ruthie's in her room, perching pink plastic hummingbird barrettes in her soft hair. Olive searches for the books she needs me to return to the library.

"Waffles?" I call out, passing their bedrooms.

"Yum!" Ruthie bounces toward the bathroom. "I just have to brush my teeth first."

In the kitchen, Abel is sitting on a stool at the island, a mug of coffee in hand. "Hope you don't mind I made a pot."

I kiss the top of his head because for the first time in a year, I can. "Mind? I feel like I'm at a luxury hotel."

"You've been to a hotel?" Abel asks, curiosity piqued. He grew up on a compound in the middle of Nowhere, Eastern Washington. The only vacations he knows are the rare camping trips we took to Moses Lake in the blazing hot summers.

Pouring myself coffee, I tell him about the motel the girls and I lived at for several months before we landed this rental. "It was definitely not luxury. But wouldn't that be fun? To stay a hotel with a swimming pool and room service?"

Abel grins. "Yeah, with palm trees and coconuts. Like in *The Swiss Family Robinson.* I loved that book when I was kid, one of the few Dad let us have."

I sigh before talking a sip of coffee, remembering the bookcase of classics that were permitted on the compound. "Sounds more like paradise."

"That's what Dad says he is building," Abel says, giving the conversation a weight I wasn't prepared for.

"Your dad says a lot of things," I say, pulling the waffle iron from the cupboard. "But how about we eat some breakfast before we talk theology?"

As the girls find their way to the kitchen, they begin peppering their big brother with questions about their half-siblings. After a year apart, they are desperate for some stories about the kids they grew up with.

I divide my attention between them and making the waffles, my mind on my work schedule, and even though I want to skip out on my shift at the library, I know I can't. I have to keep my job if I want to keep my family together. And now that I don't have extra income from wELLEness, I need to double down with the job I do have.

"And Naomi's baby cries all the time. But she is already praying every night at dinner for God to bless her with another," Abel is saying.

I bite back a comment that would sound bitter, because under that emotion is sorrow. Loss. I miss my sister wives even though both Naomi and Lydia drove me crazy at times. My relationship with them was much deeper than I will ever have with the ladies in the neighborhood. We shared a home, a kitchen—a man. We were a family. A family I tore apart.

"Okay, eat up, and then get your coats, girls. It's freezing out, and we have to be at the library in thirty minutes."

"Why do we have to come?" Olive asks as she pours more syrup on her golden waffles.

"Because I am not asking Sophie to babysit one more time this week. Or her mother. And I am not leaving you both home alone all day."

"I'll be here," Abel says. "And I'll be sixteen in a few weeks. Surely old enough to babysit. You were younger than I am when you gave birth to me."

I wince. The memory, while true, is hard to accept. I wasn't just a teenage bride, I was a teen mom. It's impossible not to be angry about all that was taken from me.

"Please, can we stay?" Ruthie asks. "Please?"

I do my best to be rational, to hear them out. To listen. We make a compromise, Ruthie and Olive can stay with Abel while I'm at work, but they won't leave the house. I don't need the neighbors trying to work out why a teenage boy is now at my house. Last night was awkward enough, going to Luna's for the girls without explaining why we were in a rush. "There's one more condition," I say. "I need a photo of my kids, together." I have the three of them pose, but I zoom in on Abel for a second picture. I make sure his face fills the screen.

When I get to work, I quickly become lost in the monotony of shelving books. It's why I love working here so much. I can keep my head down and my worry at bay. Tarin, my coworker, asks me to bring a cart of books into a meeting room reserved by a local book club. She is preparing for the meeting that starts in a few minutes.

When I enter the large room filled with a circle of folding chairs, I smile, seeing Julia, my neighbor. She's sitting next to Granger, another neighbor who just bought the gray house on the corner.

"It's so good to see you, Gray," Julia says, walking over and giving me a quick hug. After the group texts this morning, I know she's up to date on my life, and she quickly fills in Granger. My cheeks burn at her description. *She caught an actual murderer.* "Oh, Kendall is here too." Julia laughs. "Thank God. I thought she might not show, which would have annoyed me considering she's the one who told me to join."

"I didn't realize you were a part of the book club," I say, looking at Tarin handing out a paper with discussion questions.

"Granger is the reader. Convinced Kendall, who convinced me." Julia smiles as Kendall joins us.

I nod. "We should put a Little Free Library in the neighborhood. That would be cool, right?"

Julia nods. "Oh, we could all make one for our yards. Wouldn't that be so cute?"

"The cutest." I smile. "Wish I could stay, but I have to get back to work. Talk soon, and nice to see you, Granger."

I leave them to it and head back to work. I call the house, and thankfully Olive picks up, letting me know they just had lunch and are looking for a movie. "Abel has never seen anything on Netflix. Can we watch *Stranger Things*?"

After explaining it's too scary for Ruthie, she relents. "Another time, Olive. Pick something PG, please."

Other mothers might not find pleasure in such a simple exchange with their children, but it was these normal conversations I longed for when I left Garden Temple. I wouldn't trade them for the world.

An hour later I'm checking out books to patrons when Granger gets to the front of the line with a pile of books.

"It's good to see you again, Granger," I say as he hands me his library card. I scan, seeing he has been in three times this week. "Looks like Julia wasn't exaggerating that you're a reader."

He smiles shyly, and I realize he might be

nervous. "Yeah, books have always been my favorite escape."

"I like that," I say, not telling him that my love for books has come late in life. It's only been this past year that I could read freely. I begin checking out his books. A how-to guide on backyard chicken coops, a book on easy origami, a new nonfiction on Napoleon. "Looks like you have a lot of interests."

He shrugs. "I'm new to town, trying to keep myself busy."

"Well, I can certainly relate to that. I've only lived in Tacoma a year."

Granger picks up his books. "Well, I'm glad we're both in the neighborhood." His hazel eyes meet mine, and I wonder for a split second if he is the sort of man who would suit me. He is unlike Jeremiah in every conceivable way. And unlike Boone, too, with his rumpled suit and pine-green eyes and his scruffy jawline. His hand on mine, his words echoing in my ear: *Call me if you need me. If you need anything at all.*

I wish calling for help was as simple as that. But it's not.

Eight hours later, I leave the library. It's nearing five o'clock, and I call the house once more. "Can you make chili?" I ask Abel. "There are cans of kidney beans in the pantry. And diced tomatoes. Olive can help. And can you ask the girls to tidy the house?"

"We're on it. Ruthie is sweeping now, and Olive is switching laundry. You trained us well," he says.

"Thank you," I say, grateful for their collective responsibility. "I have a few stops to make, then I'll be home, okay?"

The sky is growing dark by the time I finish my errands. Once I pull into the driveway at home, I let my shoulders fall. Being home has never sounded so appealing. Ever since I found Patrick dead, my life has been racing. Thankfully, I have the next two days off from work. Besides dealing with Abel's Bethany crisis, which I have no idea how to handle. I plan on catching up on meal plans and laundry.

Inside the house I find a pot of chili burning on the stove, and the back door wide open, the porch lights on.

Pulse quickening, I flick off the burner. "Hello?" I call. "Where is everyone?"

No answer. No sound.

"Abel? Ruthie? Olive?" I shout, heading straight to the open door. "Are you out there?"

Then I hear them.

"Ruthie! Where are you?" Abel is yelling, Olive too. "Ruthie, it isn't funny! Come inside!"

"What's happening?" My voice is more than ragged, raw. It's laced with absolute terror. Olive and Abel turn, eyes wide, filled with fear.

"She took out the trash fifteen minutes ago," Abel says, walking closer to me, out of breath. "And we haven't seen her since."

3

Outside, the mid-February air is icy, crisp. Snow is threatening to fall. The sky is cloudless, inky black, as expansive as my fear.

I turn in a circle, then another, searching for my girl. My girl who likes her milk with ice, and peanut butter in her ice cream, who's afraid of spiders and sleeps with a night-light.

My little girl. My girl. Mine.

"Tell me exactly what happened," I say, my voice shaking as I turn to Olive and Abel.

"You called," Abel says. "You told me you were on your way home. I was making chili; Olive went to the basement to run laundry. And Ruthie offered to take out the trash after she finished sweeping. I even saw her turn the back porch light on. It was only one bag."

I walk around the side of the house to where the garbage bins are stored. I open one up and see a new bag on top, with the pizza box from last night. She got the trash here, but then what?

"Maybe she went to Cleo's?" Olive suggests, her voice betraying her feelings. Cracked.

"Okay, yes." I nod, wanting to believe it is as simple as going to a friend's house, even though Ruthie knows better than to leave like that. "I'll go over there."

Ruthie may have just wanted to see her classmate. Cleo's mom, Julia, who I saw a few hours ago at the library, lives only a few doors down. I tell Olive and Abel to start looking on the street.

But Julia's home is pitch dark; the family's SUV isn't in the driveway. I knock, but nothing. I pull out my phone, realizing I can cut to the chase with the group chat.

ME: ***Hey, is Ruthie at one of your homes?***

STRAIGHT TO THE POINT, no games. A simple question that will tell me, quite possibly, more than I can handle. I stare at the phone screen, running back toward my house. A moment later it pings once, then twice.

JULIA: ***No, we went to Spiral's for meatball subs. Bart's favorite Headed to the arcade after. Anyone wanna join?***

HER HUSBAND, Bart, is a nice man. I can imagine him loading the kids and his wife into their Suburban on a Friday night, getting sandwiches, and handing out quarters. Smiles on the faces of every member of their perfect family unit. Tears burn my eyes, jealousy weaving its way to my heart.

I tighten my jaw, ruling out one friend's house.

KENDALL: ***Sorry I don't have your sweet pea. Last minute plan—drove to my in-laws in Port Orchard this afternoon. A mini getaway for the 3-day weekend. XOXO***

. . .

LUNA: ***I'm at Ohh La La, stocking up on essentials in case we get a blizzard. But Sophie is home—maybe she has Ruthie?? Are you worried? Where's Olive??***

ESSENTIALS AT OHH LA LA? It's a wine shop downtown. But not wanting to cast judgment, I brush it aside and reply.

ME: ***Okay, headed over to see if she's w/Sophie now. I have Olive. Probably nothing. She just took out the trash and didn't come back inside. It's been 15 minutes.***

A RUSH of shame washes over me as I reread the sentence now displayed on the phone screen. Am I a bad parent for not knowing where my eight-year-old is? Yes. Irrevocably yes.

"I'm going see if Sophie's seen her," I tell the kids as I pass our driveway. They trail along with me, clearly scared of being left alone. I want someone at the house in case Ruthie returns, but I don't want either of them out of my sight either.

I knock on Luna's door, still decorated with a heart wreath. Valentine's Day was only a few days ago, but it suddenly feels like the time for sweet treats and love notes is long gone. Where is my daughter?

"Hi, Gray. My mom isn't here," Sophie says as she answers the door. She's in very short shorts and a thin tank top, her long hair piled on the top of her head. Looking over my shoulder, she waves. "Hey, Olive, and—" She frowns, not recognizing Abel. "Who's that?" she asks me.

"That is, uh, Olive's brother, Abel." I smile tightly, not saying the word *son*. Because a woman on the brink of thirty should not have a son nearly grown. Should she? "But I wasn't looking for your mom. I was wondering if Ruthie is here."

"Ruthie?" Sophie frowns. "No. I haven't seen her since last night."

My face must be written with worry because Sophie's now asking what's wrong.

My phone buzzes. So does the one in Sophie's hand. The texts are coming in, fast.

JULIA: ***Is she with Sophie?***

Kendall: ***This is worrying me. How long has it been???***

SOPHIE READS HER TEXTS TOO, which I am guessing are from her mother. Then she reaches out, startling me, taking hold of my wrist. "You should call the police, Gray. Ruthie isn't here. Which means..."

I swallow, nodding, blinking back tears, arriving at the same conclusion. Wondering what kind of mother I am if a teenager knew what to do before I did.

"If you hear anything," I say. "Anything at all."

Sophie nods, looking at Olive. "Of course."

I walk down the front steps of her home, and Olive silently takes my hand. Inside our house, I do a thorough search, upstairs and down, in the basement. The garage. Every closet, behind every couch. Thinking of my children as toddlers, how games of hide-and-seek would entertain them for hours. I remember once, Lydia's daughter was hiding in a garden shed, and we spent hours looking for her. Once found, she got a through lesson from her father about how it was not okay to waste people's time with childish games. But she was four. Ruthie is eight. She's too old for a game of cat and mouse that go on so long.

The house is empty save for the three of us. Ruthie is not here.

Olive and Abel are realizing that too, and panic is setting in. I need to take control of the situation before they fall apart.

"I'm calling for help," I tell them. I turn from them, phone in hand. More texts have come in on the group chat, but I have nothing more to say. Biting my bottom lip, I search my contacts, press call, and pray he picks up the phone.

A moment later, his gruff voice comes through. "Gray? Didn't expect to hear from—"

I cut him off, desperate now as I realize the gravity of the situation. "Boone, I need help. Ruthie's gone. We're at home, but I can't find her. Please. Can you—"

"I'm already in my car," he says, not asking for an explanation. "I'll be there. Hold on."

I end the call, turning to the kids. "Boone is on his way," I say. "He'll know what to do."

"Boone?" Abel asks.

Olive nods, relieved. "He's a detective. And Mom's friend."

"A cop?" Abel's eyebrows raise, and I understand why. We've lived our life under the radar. On the compound we were taught that outside authorities are always in the wrong. Now I am inviting one into our home.

"He's a good man," I say, wanting to believe that Orion Boone, a man I've known, what, a few weeks, is who he says he is. Solid. True. Trustworthy.

Still, I have reason to be apprehensive.

"Listen, Abel, I don't want him to know about Garden Temple. About our past."

His brows shoot up. "Why is that?" he asks.

"Because I'm not interested in causing problems for the people we all love. Not like this. And besides, the focus needs to be on Ruthie right now, not your father's cult."

"Cult?" Abel tenses. "Is that what you're calling it? I thought it was the guiding light, the truth? My father is a prophet. You're the first wife of the most holy man and I—"

"Stop," Olive shouts at him. "Are you seriously going to defend the person who is marrying the girl you love at a time like this?"

Abel snorts. "It's not as black and white as

that, Olive. But you wouldn't understand considering you're not a man."

"Enough!" Now it's my turn to shout. "We aren't talking about Garden Temple! We are talking about Ruthie." I'm not one to raise my voice, but this—them fighting like this—will not work. Not for one more second. And right now it's seconds that matter. Their little sister, my daughter, is nowhere to be found.

There is a knock on the door. I give the kids a stern look and then walk to the door. When I pull it open, I start to cry. No longer blinking back tears, I let them fall down my cheeks as this strong man wraps me in his arms.

"Hey, it's okay. I got you," he says as I cry against his chest. In this moment, I choose to believe him. I need it to be okay.

When the flood of emotion subsides, I step back, inviting Boone inside. The porch lamp falls over his face, the warm glow picking up the shadows of the snow now coming down outside. Was Ruthie dressed for a snowstorm? Was she even wearing shoes?

"The snow came in fast," I say, my voice cracking as I close the door behind us.

"We're not talking weather. Gray, tell me what you know. Where could Ruthie be?"

I lead him into the living room where Abel and Olive are pacing. "This is my son, Abel," I tell Boone. "He just came into town last night. He lives in Eastern Washington with his dad."

Boone's eyes take in my son, and while I had thought Abel was nearly fully grown, next to Boone he looks more like a child than a teenager.

"Good to meet you," Boone says, offering a handshake.

Abel steps closer, taking it. "Ruthie was here," he says. "Mom was working, and I was watching the girls, and she took out the trash and then never came back inside. I don't what happened."

"When was that?" Boone asks.

"Thirty minutes ago," he answers.

Boone's jaw tightens; his eyes find mine. "Tell me everything."

There isn't much to say, but I give him the rundown of looking outside, in the house, the neighbors Ruthie knows.

"I'm calling in York and Truce. We need to find her. Now." Boone pulls out his phone, walking to the kitchen, phone to his ear. I pick up some words.

Missing ... eight years old ... Gray from the wELLEness case.

When he walks back into the living room, I ask what happens next.

"Next? Next, we find your daughter, Gray. Next, we bring Ruthie home."

"Maybe she just wandered off down the street."

"Thirty minutes ago? In the dark, when it's snowing?"

I shake my head, and Olive falls into the armchair, crying. "Where would she go?"

"Go?" Abel shakes his head. "No. The question is who took her."

Olive's head snaps up. "Like kidnapped?"

"Oh God, don't say that," I say. "It's going to be fine. She's probably..." I can't even finish the sentence; it's hollow, and everyone in the room knows it. Boone may not understand the bounds of the secrets the girls and I have kept this last year, but I do. And I know Ruthie would never play games like this.

While I wait for more officers to arrive, I tell the neighborhood ladies what's happening via text, that we've called in the police. Worried messages immediately light up my screen, but I focus on Boone. He tells me he is going to go through the house again, if that's all right.

"Of course. Look everywhere."

Soon, Truce and York are here, officers I met the morning I found Patrick dead in his condo. Now, they seem like friends.

"What do we do?" I ask the room.

Boone tells me to sit down. "I need to get an initial report taken down, Gray. I know Ruthie, but we need this on file so everyone can help."

I nod, appreciating how direct Boone is with me. "Of course, what do you need to know exactly?"

Boone clears his throat. "Her height, her appearance"—then looking over at Olive and Abel—"and I need to know what she was wearing when she left the house to take out the trash. Any detail you can remember whatsoever."

Olive speaks up, rubbing at her eyes. "She was so excited for it to start snowing. She was talking about it through the entire movie we'd just watched. She put on her puffy coat and that pink scarf you knit her, Mom."

"And how tall is Ruthie, her eye color?" Boone asks. "And we need a photo."

I take a deep breath and begin to talk quickly, realizing with every word I say, we are using these seconds on something other than looking for my little girl. Realizing that time is not on our side. Maybe it never has been.

4

As we finish giving Boone information for the missing-child report, a uniformed woman arrives at my doorstep. Her dark hair is in a tight bun at the base of her neck, and her demeanor is serious, intense, but her eyes tell me she cares. I appreciate having a female patrol officer with me. After being a sister wife for so long, I've always gotten along with women.

"I'm Officer Charlie Callahan," she tells me. "This neighborhood is on my patrol. While York and Truce are great officers, I know this area very well. Boone and I are going to be helping you at the ground level."

"I understand," I say, an arm around Olive.

"Is there another parent we can interview to get a better picture of what is going on here?" Callahan asks me.

I shake my head. "No, my husband and I have been separated for a year. He lives across the mountains. He has no contact with the girls."

Boone frowns. "But your son, Abel, he just got into town last night?"

I nod, looking over at my boy, suddenly thinking the absolute worst.

He said the letter Olive had sent him with our whereabouts had been kept hidden, but was he being honest with me? Did he have something to do with this?

"I came alone," Abel says. "I needed some space from my dad."

"And he knew this?" Boone asks.

Abel clenches his jaw, runs a hand through his short hair. "No, I mean, I left without saying anything."

Boone makes a note, and Callahan keeps talking. "Do you and your children's father have a custody agreement on file with a specific county?"

I shake my head. "No. Nothing formal. We were never even legally married, let alone divorced." My cheeks burn at this admission, and I wonder if Boone thinks I'm a liar. I know for a fact I've used the word "ex-husband" around him. This is why you don't tell white lies. Everything can come back to haunt you.

"And your daughter Ruthie—what was her pattern of behavior?" Callahan continues. "Has she ever left like this before?"

"No, never. She's a good girl. She knew I was on my way home."

"Anything else you can remember?" Callahan asks the kids. "I understand your mom was at work. What were you and your brother and sister doing, Olive?"

"We got in a fight," Olive says, biting her bottom lip. "The three of us. After the movie. Abel told us to clean the house since we were the girls. And I told him no, that he should do the dishes. And Ruthie got upset, started crying, saying she didn't want to listen to us fight. That she wanted us to be nice to one another, to clean the house before Mom got home. We apologized, knowing she was all worked up, but she was still crying as she swept the kitchen. She said that tomorrow she was going to make a snowman because a snowman friend would never fight like we did." She is trembling by the time she finishes, and I wrap my arms around her, understanding her pain.

Callahan makes eye contact with Boone, and I wonder what silent conversation is happening. "Is that how you remember things, Abel?"

Abel nods. "Pretty much."

Truce tells us he and York will be doing a more thorough search of the house. "It's not unusual to find a child in their home. Maybe she fell asleep under a bed or something. We'll look through closets, crawl spaces, and this is an old house so the basement and attic too: you understand?"

"Of course," I say, feeling frantic. "But shouldn't we look outside?"

"We will," Callahan says. "But we need to get all of this information for the missing-persons report."

I run my hands over my face and try to focus on the questions she asks: *Are there problems at school? What places does the child frequent? Are there any family problems affecting the child? Does the child use drugs or alcohol?*

"What?" I gasp. "No. Ruthie's eight."

"I understand, ma'am, but I'm just following protocol. The next step is for me to create a file for NCIC—the National Crime

Information Center's missing-person database. From here on out, Detective Boone will be the lead investigator. But I will be here, helping lead the patrol search, along with Truce. And Officer York will work with a team from a crime analysis unit."

"What's that?" I ask, her words flying around so fast. Olive and Abel are at my side, each holding one of my hands as if grounding me in the moment. Knowing I might break.

Callahan remains calm. "The crime unit will look at school incident reports, suspicious vehicles on file, child abuse reports—"

I cut her off. "There is no abuse taking place in our home. None."

Boone steps in. "No one is saying there is, Gray. This is the investigation checklist, okay? We don't want to miss anything."

I nod, looking into his eyes. Does he think I could have hurt my little girl?

"We're going to find her, and you will have your family all back together, okay?"

Callahan clears her throat, and I wonder if it's because she doesn't like the sort of promise Boone is making. And if so, is that because it might not come true?

There's a knock on the door and we all

jump. I move to answer it, and at my steps I find my neighbors all bundled up in coats and boots because the snow is falling harder now. Julia and Bart Granger; Sophia and her mom, Luna, and her dad, Hank; Avery and her wife, Matilda; even Kendall and her husband, Craig, who had just driven to Port Orchard for the weekend. It means they turned around, came back—for Ruthie. Nearly everyone from the street is here, and that show of support hits me hard. I'm not alone in this.

"What can we do?" Luna asks. "We got sitters for the littles. We're here to help until we find Ruthie."

Tears fill my eyes, and Officer Callahan joins me at the door. "This is an incredible show of support," she says. "Officer Truce and I are going to be leading the patrol search in the neighborhood, so we can get your information right outside. We will be setting up a command post outside of the home. We will also need identification from everyone." As we stand at the front door, I see police cars pulling into the street. "At the moment, Gray and her children will be inside giving more information on Ruthie, but

Officer Truce can join you out here as we mobilize the search."

"Children?" Julia asks.

I nod. "My son, Abel—he came into town last night, for a visit."

"I didn't realize you had other children," she says, tilting her head to the side before pasting a smile on her face. "We'll find Ruthie; don't you worry, Gray."

Officer Truce takes over the crowd of volunteers. Sophie, though, pushes through into my house. "Can I talk to you, Gray?"

"What is it?" I ask, Callahan right at my side. I wonder if she is going to stay next to me as we move through this investigation, until Ruthie is home. It's a comforting idea. A stand-in sister wife.

"Maybe it's weird to mention," Sophie says, "but that guy Cody, who lives at the end of the street with his grandma, he's been acting super creepy lately."

I pull in a sharp breath. "Creepy?"

Sophie's changed from her shorts and tank top, and is now bundled up in winter clothing for a long night of searching. As a sixteen-year-old in the neighborhood, who I have entrusted my girls with multiple times, I want to hear what she has to say.

"Yeah, last week I saw him through my bedroom window just, like, staring at me. I was changing. It was totally gross."

"Did you tell your parents?"

"My dad went and talked to his grandma, but she is not exactly all there. And my mom got me blackout curtains. Anyway, my parents thought I should tell the police."

"Thank you, Sophie," Callahan says. "I'll actually get the rest of this report from you right now. Mind talking at the table?"

They walk away, and I gravitate to Olive and Abel. "You didn't say anything to your dad, did you?"

"I told you I didn't," Abel repeats. "I came for Bethany, Mom. Not for Ruthie."

Tears fill my eyes. "I know you're worried about both of them."

Abel presses his fingertips to his temples. "Right now it's Ruthie we need to focus on. I'm so sorry, Mom. I thought she could go out alone."

"She can. She does," I say, wanting to reassure him.

"Cory is a creep," Olive says. "He's always hovering around the bus stop."

"How old is he?" Abel asks.

Olive shrugs. "I think someone said he graduated last year."

"If he took her"—Abel's eyes grow dark—"I'll destroy him."

"Not the time for threats," I say firmly as more policemen and women enter my home, and York begins organizing them. I hear the words *trash can ... fingerprints ... camera footage.*

I turn to Boone, who is looking at the tablet Callahan has in her hands. "What about the cameras you installed?" I ask. "They might show something."

Boone nods. "I already gave the footage and access to the cameras to Callahan. Hopefully, we can find something on them. Only wish the camera over the back door hadn't been broken a few days ago."

Callahan looks between us. "You installed Gray's security cameras?"

Boone runs a hand over his jaw. "Yes, we're friends. Met on the wELLEness case a few weeks ago."

Callahan nods tightly. "Right, of course." Then she tilts her head to the front door. "Boone, the mobile command post is on its way. They're setting up on the empty lot on the corner. While we have other people to interview, this is, at the moment, a non-family abduction case."

"Before we go, I was going over the report, Gray, and I'm missing a few things," Boone says. "When did you leave work, and when did you get home?"

I swallow, telling myself to keep a neutral expression, a placid face. "I got off at five and ran a few errands before coming home a little after six."

Boone runs a hand over his jaw. "What errands?"

Callahan has her tablet in hand, jotting down notes as I speak, filling in the gaps.

"I went to the gas station and the, uh, bank. The cash machine."

"Anything else?" Callahan asks, her pointer finger hovering above the touch screen.

"Honestly?" I lie. "I went to the waterfront, bought a cup of tea, and just tried to think of how to deal with my teenager who just showed up on my doorstep."

"What a week you've had. God, I'm sorry." Callahan shakes her head sympathetically. My friends were murdered, my absent son returned, and my daughter went missing. I wish the stop at the water hadn't been a lie. I really would have loved a moment to just think without all of the stressors I currently face.

"Well, that answers that," Boone says.

"Are you both leaving now?" I ask, suddenly scared at the thought of being without either of them. Boone is somehow one of my closest friends in the world, and Callahan is someone I've just met, yet being in her presence makes me feel safe. And right now, I need safe. Before they answer, a man's voice cuts through my thoughts.

"Callahan, Boone," Truce calls from the door. "We found something."

Something? Not someone?

My knees give way. Boone grabs me by the waist before I meet the floor.

"Not now, Gray West. You need to stand strong," he says, his gruff voice calm in my ear. His words penetrating me deep. He's right, of course. Now isn't the time to fall apart. Now is the time to take control.

5

TRUCE HAS CROPPED black hair and a sharp nose. His demeanor is forthright, no-nonsense in a way Boone isn't. Boone has his heartstrings pulled, even if he won't admit it. He is a father who lost his daughter, and because of that I know he is invested in ways he maybe shouldn't be. Or maybe he should. Maybe Boone is the sort of detective every city needs. A man who has been through hell and back again, standing on two feet. Standing, like I am trying to stand now. With feet firmly planted, eyes wide open. Listening as Truce walks toward where we stand in the dining room. The chili still sits on the stove, charred black, and though my stomach rolls with hunger, my heart burns with fear.

"What did you find?" Callahan asks.

Olive and Abel are with us; the other officers who have been in the house and yard remain at my periphery. My eyes land on what Truce holds in his hands.

A pink scarf, hand-knit by me, a gift I had wrapped and placed under our very first Christmas tree. We never had such a sacrilegious thing at Garden Temple, a pine decorated with twinkly lights and ornaments we made sitting at our kitchen table, glitter and paper chains, trying to remember the traditions I'd had as a little girl, before my parents died, before I was taken in by my Aunt Sandy and Uncle Joseph, who lived at the compound that would forever change my life. They died several years ago; by then I was married and a mother, and though they were the reason I lived at the cult for so long, they were not the reason I fled. No, I left because I knew my daughters deserved more than what they were being offered.

They deserved a fighting chance at real happiness.

Now, the soft wool yarn is wet and muddy, held in a grown man's hands when it should be wrapped around the neck of my little girl.

"It's Ruthie's scarf," Olive cries. "Mom, it's her scarf."

"Where did you find this?" I ask. Replaying the moment I walked into the house this evening, finding Abel and Olive outside, shouting for their little sister. I had walked from the back door to the trash cans, and I didn't see this. We scoured the yard, the street. None of us saw Ruthie's scarf.

"It was in the alley behind the houses across the street," Truce tells us. "A neighbor, Luna, said it was Ruthie's, but we needed to confirm with you."

I stretch out my hand to take it, but Truce pulls back. "I'm sorry, Gray," he says. "It needs to go into evidence and get fingerprinted."

"You can do that to fabric?"

"We can try," he says. "And work on extracting DNA too."

I watch Truce and Callahan walk away, my daughter's scarf in their possession, and I feel a part of me torn away. I need to hold on to a piece of Ruthie, to believe she is still here, not taken. Not gone.

It's been ninety minutes since I came home, and I know the clock is ticking in a situation like this. If the only lead they have is a wet scarf, it's not enough to find my daughter.

I need to speak with Boone. Now.

Because I might know who took Ruthie. There is only one man who has ever been after me. And not saying something means not putting my child first. But it's a terrifying conversation to have.

"Is it wrong of us to eat?" Olive asks. "I'm so hungry."

"No, it's okay," I say, my eyes meeting Boone's. Silently willing him to stay close by, to not follow Callahan. "Why don't you make some peanut butter and jelly sandwiches? There are pretzels in the pantry."

In the kitchen I see someone made a pot of coffee, and I pour myself a mug, Boone too. Olive silently hands me creamer, and then reaches for a loaf of bread.

"Honey," I tell her, "I'm going talk to Boone upstairs for a sec, okay?"

She nods, and Abel pulls a flip phone from his pocket. My lips press together, not realizing he had a cell phone with him. No one on the compound had them. At least I didn't think they did. But maybe there were more secrets at Garden Temple than I realized. Certainly no one knew mine—that I'd killed a man before being bound to Jeremiah. That blood is on my hands, and I can never wash it away.

"Where did you get that?" I have to ask.

Abel's eyes lift. "The phone? I bought a couple for Bethany and me a few weeks ago at a gas station. No one at home knows we have them."

I nod, accepting his explanation and hoping it's the truth.

Boone doesn't press me to speak. He says something to Callahan in the living room, then follows me as I walk upstairs.

There is only one place I want to be right now.

I step inside Ruthie's bedroom as a police officer I don't know exits my bedroom. His hands are empty; I have nothing in that room to hide. The pills I had stashed in my underwear drawer were taken from this house by the very man at my heels, and the stories I've kept close to my chest can't be told unless I'm the one opening up, spilling them out.

How do you tell someone your life has not been your own? That you've been a victim since you were a child, that when given the chance to speak up, speak out, you stayed silent? How do you explain to someone that you've lived your life in constant fear without sounding weak?

And why do I care if Boone thinks I am weak anyway? Isn't it enough that *I* know I am strong?

But with him, it isn't. With him, in my daughter's bedroom, I want him to know I am capable. That I am more than a girl who said yes to a man. A man who took away many things from me but not my innocence. That was gone the night I lifted the bookend and smashed it against Bishop Timothy's head, leaving him bleeding out at my feet. Maybe it was gone before that, when I was ten years old and in a car that crashed, leaving me an orphan, my parents dead, eyes blank, looking toward a future they would never see.

We stand in quiet, and I'm guessing he's analyzing his words before he says them, same as me.

Boone is a detective; he knows the weight of confessions, of clues, of catastrophe.

I turn to him, eyes filling with tears, and I will them not to spill over, not to roll down my cheeks, because I don't want to cry, not over this, because crying now means Jeremiah still has a hold over me.

But he does, doesn't he? I may not have

seen him in a year, but he is in my head constantly, whispering lies to me about my weaknesses, about my worth. I listened for so long, I let them become my truths.

But I'm not beholden to Jeremiah anymore. Legally, I never was. I was given to him in a wedding ceremony when I was fourteen. There is no court of law that would recognize that marriage as legal, even though my guardians, my aunt and uncle, offered him my hand.

"I need to tell you something," I say, my back to Boone. I lean down to the worn wooden floorboards and pick up a pink paper crane, running my fingertips over the folds, focused on choosing my words with care. I can't undo this once it has been done. There will be no going back.

"What is it, Gray?" he asks.

"I need to tell you about Ruthie's father."

"Okay," he says slowly, running a hand over the base of his neck, as if strained. He swallows, looking at me, and I brush away the tears with the back of my hand. I want him to reach out and take it. Take me. Where? I don't know—away from my current reality. A reality where my little girl is missing, and I might know why.

"What do you want me to know?" he asks.

Maybe I should have brought Callahan up here with me. A woman I just met, who doesn't know I am hiding my past. Boone reaches out and takes my hand. Squeezes it. I don't let go.

"I want you to know that he might have had something to do with Ruthie being taken. He is volatile, and can't be trusted. When I left with the girls, I didn't tell him I was leaving."

"Did Abel know?"

I shake my head. "No. Abel stayed behind. I didn't tell him I was leaving either." I exhale slowly. "You might think I'm a terrible mother for leaving without my son but—"

"I don't think you're a terrible mother, Gray. I think you are a survivor."

I wish the timing was different, that I had moments to waste to allow those words to sink in, but I don't. Ruthie doesn't.

"I might be wrong, but my husband is the only person who has a grudge against me. And Jeremiah knows now that Abel left home, and if he knows where we are ... he could have followed."

"How did Abel know where to find you?"

"You know those weird things you noticed here, the Coke bottle and open door? It was Abel. He came a few times trying to muster up the courage to stay. Olive had sent him a letter telling him where we moved." I exhale, scared of the question I know is on the tip of Boone's tongue.

"Do you think Abel had a role in Ruthie's disappearance?"

My chest caves in on itself; my shoulders fall forward. I pull my hand from his, dropping my face in my palms. "I don't know, Boone. But I had to say something. In case."

"You're doing the right thing, Gray. I need you to come speak with Charlie, uh, Callahan, with me and tell her the contact information for Jeremiah."

"He lives five hours away," I say, panic rising as I think things through. "If he has Ruthie, he'll be on the road. And what if he has nothing to do with this? I'll never forgive myself if I get everyone looking one place for her, and she's somewhere else."

"That isn't how it works. This situation has already escalated, and state law enforcement is involved. We will track down Jeremiah and continue our search here." He pauses. "A father has a right to know his daughter is in danger."

I nod, feeling more steady from this explanation. "Okay, I'll go talk to Callahan."

"Good, and if I'm not around for a few hours, and you need me, call me, okay?"

"Thank you," I say, wanting to do more than squeeze his hand. I want to hug him, like I did when he showed up at my door. But I don't give in to my roller coaster of emotions; instead I walk with him back to the living room, looking for Callahan.

I will give her the facts she needs to get to Jeremiah but not the ugly truth of how I came to have his children. That conversation isn't for a night like this. A night when there is already so much on the line.

6

For a night I expected to drag on forever, it somehow passes too quickly. Olive cries herself to sleep, and I sit with her, calming her down. The guilt of the sibling argument is eating at her. Abel is questioned at the kitchen table for an hour. But he offers up his cell phone, and the only calls and texts are with Bethany. Thankfully, he cooperates and willingly tells the officers what bus he took into town and when. And I know the guilt is wrecking him too. He falls asleep, sitting at the table, head resting in his arms, and I let him be, thankful he and Olive at least are finding time to rest.

Me, I'm a wreck. Pacing the house, waiting for dawn to break, for a pink light to appear across the horizon so the local search can truly begin. I've been told family is not allowed to help with the ground search, so I feel locked in this house. The only place I'm allowed to go is the command post in the empty gas station parking lot.

By now I am sure a unit has made it to the compound, to Jeremiah, and I wish in some ways I could have given him warning. But I didn't, couldn't. If there is any chance Jeremiah has Ruthie there, I need him caught off guard.

A search coordinator has made a grid and is working on mobilizing the non-police personnel, dividing them into squads. My friends in the neighborhood set up a coffee table for volunteers. They will need something to keep them warm considering the freezing temperatures outside. The snow has been falling heavily, and there is a foot accumulated.

If there was ever a terrible night for this to happen, this is it. It will make searching, and finding clues, all the more difficult.

The congregation from the church Julia attends is here, and it's not even 5 a.m. Several news crews are on the street, their vans parked under street lamps, and

Callahan comes up to me with a uniformed man I haven't met yet.

"Gray, this is Fillippe. He is the media specialist assigned to this case, and he would like to speak to you."

I shake his hand, my head in a fog of worry and fear. It's been ten hours since Ruthie took out the trash. Ten hours since my world screeched to a grinding halt.

"I want to talk with you about doing an interview. The morning news is airing soon, and this would be a chance to tell viewers exactly what is happening."

I tense. "Me? Wouldn't people prefer to hear form the police?"

"Not in abduction cases. Hearing a heartfelt message from the family goes a long way and would mean mobilizing more people in the area to look for your daughter."

"Aren't officers already going door to door?"

"Yes, but an interview could help, maybe tip off a local resident to call in something suspect they saw last night."

I shake my head. I don't want to be on camera, my face and family plastered in the media. I've spent the last year scared of being found, and the idea of just putting myself out there terrifies me. If it wasn't Jeremiah who took Ruthie, he would find out where we are.

"I don't know," I say, rubbing my eyes. Fillippe frowns, clearly not anticipating this reaction.

Callahan clears her throat. "You know, Gray, this would be a good time to take a quick shower, change, get something to eat. You need to take care of yourself."

My reaction is to resist, but she restates her suggestion. "You won't be good for anyone if you aren't able to keep your eyes open. I'm not suggesting a five-hour nap. I'm saying wash your face and eat some toast, okay?"

Taking her advice, I head upstairs, knowing that since I am not allowed to be assigned to a search grid, there isn't much they will let me do. It makes sense why I can't go. They've established that parents are frequently the abductors in cases involving young children. Yes, I put Jeremiah's name out there as a possibility, but I am not naïve to the fact they may just as well be thinking I have something to do with this. They wouldn't be doing their job if they didn't also look at me.

I turn on the shower, making sure the

bathroom door is locked. Stepping out of my clothes, I try to avoid looking in the mirror. But I catch a glimpse of myself. Of my bloodshot eyes, the dark circles under them, my hair in a ponytail. I pull out the elastic and run my fingers through my scalp, thinking, as I do, of Ruthie.

A song fills my mind and I sing it, my voice a whisper, the hallowed prayer all I have to give. I may have left the church, but the words have stayed in the recesses of my mind, and I return to them now, even if unconsciously.

"Let not your heart be troubled," His tender word I hear,

And resting on His goodness I lose my doubts and fears,

Tho' by the path He leadeth, but one step I may see,

His eye is on the sparrow, and I know He watches me;

His eye is on the sparrow, and I know He watches me.

. . .

What does it mean, in my time of brokenness, that I turn to a song that's bound to a faith I no longer cling to? What does it mean that in my time of need, I go back to my where my story began to unravel? Only that what offers us comfort is not something we choose; it is something we learn over time.

I wash my body, my hair, and brush my teeth. With a towel wrapped around me, I open the door, needing to get to my room to change into fresh clothes. Thankfully, the house is quiet, and I enter my room, grateful for another moment to think, alone.

I pull on jeans and a sweater, thick socks, and boots. I know I won't be allowed to search, but I plan to go to the command post and find out if anyone has gotten ahold of Jeremiah. Of course, if they found him with Ruthie, I would already know. But what if he is hiding her? The compound is a large place. It might be a while before there is a clear answer.

A knock on the door startles me, then Olive calls out. "Mom?"

"Come in," I say, running a comb through my hair as she comes in and sits on my bed. She has changed her clothes too, and I see Abel a few steps behind her. He hands me a mug of coffee, and I take a sip. He opens his palm, offering me a bottle of ibuprofen, and I groan, thankful for it. "My head is pounding," I say.

"Boone brought it over, and some donuts."

"Is he still here?"

Abel shakes his head. "No, he seems really tense. Which, doesn't make me feel very good."

"I know. It feels like time is running out." I set my coffee down on the top of my dresser and pour out the tablets, swallowing four quickly.

"Maybe the police are talking to that Cory guy?" Olive says. "Maybe he ..."

"You really think a teenager would take a little girl?" Abel asks.

She shrugs. "I don't know. I don't know anything. I'm just ... really scared."

"I am too," I admit, wrapping my arms around her. "The police want me to talk to the reporters; they say it might bolster the community to rally behind us and help look for Ruthie."

"Are you going to?" Abel asks.

"I said no at first. I got scared about the cameras, but what do you think?"

Just then a phone rings, and Abel pulls his out. "It's Bethany," he says.

"Answer it," I say, breathless. Maybe she knows something.

"Hey," he says into the phone, then immediately puts the call on speakerphone. That action wipes away some of my doubts of him. That he had something to do with this. I reach for my coffee and gulp it down, wishing I hadn't considered him a suspect.

"Abel? The police are here at the compound. Everyone is freaking out."

"Do you know why?" he asks.

"No, no one does. They took the prophet. Do you know why?"

"Did he have anyone ..." Abel looks to me, as if unsure of what to say, how much to let on.

"Bethany," I say. "It's me, Grace. Is there any way you could go to Naomi and give her the phone?"

"Naomi?" Bethany pauses. "She's not here. She left yesterday morning."

"What do you mean, left?" I ask. Naomi is Jeremiah's third and youngest wife. First there was me, then Lydia, then Naomi. Next will be Bethany.

"She went to see Tracy in Spokane. She's

having a baby. Naomi's helping with her other kids while she gives birth."

It's very unusual for any of Jeremiah's wives to leave the compound, but I remember Naomi leaving to be with her half sister for her other labors. "Who drove her?"

"I don't know. I think she drove herself. Want me to ask?" Bethany offers.

"Can you get Lydia on the phone for me?" I ask her. Lydia and I have never gotten on well, but with Naomi gone, she is in the house alone. If Jeremiah was with her yesterday, then he wasn't abducting his daughter.

"Uh, yeah, I'm outside. It will just be a minute, but she'll be upset I have a cell phone."

"I know, but it's okay. Tell her it is Abel's fault if she asks, okay?"

Abel's eyes widen, but he doesn't argue.

"Maybe you can call her at her house?" Bethany says.

The home I used to share with Lydia is the only one on the compound with a house phone, because it's the prophet's house. Bethany is clearly worried about being in trouble for the contraband and wants me to try Lydia myself.

"It's okay," I tell her. "Believe me. Right

now, I need to talk to her, and I don't want the children in the household to know she's getting a call."

"Okay," Bethany relents. "Just a second."

I imagine her walking through her backyard, along the gravel path that leads to the prophet's home. She would be passing our church, the schoolhouse, the supply shed. There are a dozen small houses on the compound, and some trailers and mobile homes set on cement blocks. It's a fragile ecosystem that subsists on government handouts and our husband's manual labor, and the money that members donate when they join the fold.

"Are you okay?" Abel asks Bethany, cutting through my memories, and I wish his focus was on Ruthie, but I know his worries are greater than that. "Did you give any thought to leaving?"

"I told you I'm not sure," Bethany says. At this, it's *my* eyes that widen. I was under the impression Bethany was hoping to escape. But maybe she doesn't want to go. Maybe Abel made this plan up without her consent. "I don't want to leave my sisters, or my parents. They are so happy about me marrying the pro—"

"You have to make a choice eventually. Time's running out, Beth. Me or my father?" Abel's voice is raised and I will help him to calm down. The last thing I need is a teenage boy acting spontaneously. Right now we need calm; we need order. We need hope that Ruthie will be found, safe and sound.

"Lydia?" I hear Bethany's voice through the phone, speaking to my sister wife. "I hoped you'd be up."

"Everyone is up; they took Jeremiah. Put him in a police car. No one knows why. Why are you here? Did he tell *you* something?"

Even through the cell phone, hundreds of miles away, I can hear her tone. The seething anger just below the surface. Her husband is taking on a new wife, usurping her once more.

"He didn't tell me anything," Bethany tells Lydia. "But Grace is on the phone. She wants to talk to you."

"Where did you get this?" Lydia asks, her voice sharp.

"It doesn't matter right now." Bethany's tone is defiant. "She knows what's happening with the prophet. At least I think she does."

"Grace?" Lydia's voice comes on the

phone. “What’s happening? The police came; he was in his office.”

“When?”

“They came about two hours ago.”

I do the math. If Jeremiah was home, was there time for him to get Ruthie back? Could she be on the compound now?

I think yes. Hours, minutes, seconds count. If she was taken at six last night, and I told Boone about Jeremiah around eight, and the police didn’t arrive on the compound until much later, he might have made it. It could be a four-hour drive if he were driving fast.

I should have spoken up the very moment Ruthie went missing.

“Did he have Ruthie with him? Was he alone? Is Ruthie there?”

“Ruthie? What? No. We have been praying all night, for our Eden. Not Ruthie. Our time is drawing near, Grace.”

“Eden?”

“Yes, our Garden is growing, and the time is coming. Grace, you should come home. Be with us.”

“Home? What are you talking about? I need to know if Ruthie is there.”

“Ruthie is always here.”

"What does that mean she's *there*?"

"In spirit, sister. As are you."

"Lydia, listen, please, listen," I say, my voice starched and thin as is my patience. "I don't know where Ruthie is. I need you to call me at this number if you hear of anything."

"I do know where she is."

"What?"

"I told you, she is with us in spirit." The call ends, and I stare at the phone in my hands.

"I need to talk to Boone and Callahan," I say to Abel and Olive. "Tell them what Lydia just said. I know there are police involved on the eastern side of the state, but they don't know how unhinged your father is. How much control he has. How—" My words get lost in the sobs that overwhelm me, and my children wrap me up in their arms.

The reality of Ruthie truly being gone hits me in a place that hurts beyond all understanding. And I know what I must do.

Keeping my mouth shut may have been what kept me safe at Garden Temple all those years, but I'm not there anymore. Being a woman who doesn't speak up no longer serves me. Now it's time to use my voice.

7

When I enter the kitchen, Callahan greets me. Like she was waiting for me.

"I can give the interviews. I want to," I tell her. "But there are some things I need to say first. So you understand my hesitancy. I know what you're thinking."

"And what's that?"

"That I'm hiding something. Not being completely forthright."

"Is that an accurate representation of the truth?" Charlie Callahan is poised to question me, and she should. I haven't told her everything.

"It is. I know I told you where I was in the hour between leaving work and coming home, but that's not what happened."

"You didn't go to the bank and the waterfront?"

I shake my head. "No, I went to the Larchmont Motel."

She frowns, considering the location I just gave her. The implications it carries. It's the roughest part of Tacoma, and that motel has a reputation—and not a good one.

I reach for a donut on the counter—the ones Boone brought—realizing how relieved I am that he isn't here right now, listening to me. I can tell Charlie Callahan the truth because she is a stranger.

I want Boone to continue to see me as he does now, as a strong woman fighting for her family, instead of a woman who is hiding, scared of being found out.

Maybe it is ridiculous to grasp on to this idea though, because that will all change soon enough. He will know. So will my neighbors, my newfound friends. They will all know the truth.

"I was at the Larchmont getting a fake ID and birth certificate for Abel. I want him to stay here, in Tacoma. With me. I knew I'd need them to get him into school. And I know it's a long shot because he might still want to go back to his father. The thing is, the father of my children is Jeremiah Priest."

"Right," she says, nodding along as she records all of this, everything I am saying, on her device between us on the kitchen counter. "You told us Jeremiah's name and his address earlier. The police in Grant County are questioning him right now. They've been with him for several hours."

"I know I told you his name, but I didn't explain just how dangerous Jeremiah is."

"Did he hurt you?" she asks.

"Not in the way you think. If he had Ruthie, or at least offered Ruthie up, I would already know about it. But Jeremiah is cunning and calculated. He doesn't do anything without thinking it through. Did the officers in Grant County tell you what they found when they brought him in for questioning?"

"I can't discuss it with you, Gray. But it's grim out there. A compound of sorts, houses and buildings, and it appears a lot of people in the area support him."

"It's not support. It's belief. Jeremiah is their prophet. The people living there will give their lives to protect him."

Charlie Callahan looks me straight in the

eyes. "The investigation here in Tacoma is just as vital as the one in Eastern Washington. We have no substantive evidence that Jeremiah has Ruthie. Until we do, we need to continue our search here, with relentless determination. Minutes count."

"I know," I say, my voice firm. "I know that. That is why I am here, talking to you. Telling you where I really was and also telling you why I was scared when Fillippe mentioned an on-camera interview. I've been hiding from Jeremiah for the last year. He controlled me for fifteen years, and even after I left, I've been walking on pins and needles, scared he might show up and ruin the life I am trying to build for my girls. So I'm scared of him knowing where I am." I pull in a sharp breath. "But I realize I'm more scared of never seeing my daughter again. So put me on camera; let me say my piece. If my daughter is here, locally, then we will find her. And if she's there, with him, I pray we put an end to all of Jeremiah's madness."

BEFORE I HEAD OUTSIDE for the interview, I tell Callahan everything that Lydia said on the phone. Her cryptic words about home, about Ruthie being with her.

"I don't know if it means anything," I say. "But tell the detectives who are at the compound. It might help."

Olive joins me in the kitchen, bringing me my winter coat and a beanie for my head. "It's freezing outside," she says. "There are so many people on the street."

"Cameras are everywhere," Abel says, pulling on his winter coat and gloves too. "And Bethany won't answer the phone now. She might have had it confiscated."

If she's in trouble for the contraband, she might be locked in a bedroom for days. And we don't have days. Not if she is set to marry Jeremiah at the end of the week.

Callahan hears that and makes another note on her tablet. At this point I don't even care—my secrets are out of the bag.

"Channel Three is ready for you," Fillippe tells me. "Want to go over the script one more time?"

"Show a photo of Ruthie; ask for help. Tell them we've been in hiding for a year and that Ruthie deserves to be home. Right?"

Fillippe nods. "Perfect." He motions for me to follow, and I step outside, my children at my side. Everyone turns to look, and I reach for Abel and Olive's hands.

"Tomas is here with his mom," Olive says, her voice quiet, as she scans the crowd, spotting her classmate and close friend.

"I'm glad you have support, Olive," I tell her, glancing at her classmate, thinking of their friendship. Reminded of Abel and Bethany's, when they were younger, before everything became so twisted.

It doesn't take long for a cameraman to get a few feet from me, a reporter at my side. "I'm so sorry," she says. "You are being so brave to do this at a time that is so terrifying."

I don't answer because I don't know what words to use. I see my neighbors Julia and Luna looking on, arms linked, watching, giving me small, tender waves. There are police officers everywhere, search units in groups marching off in different directions. My heart breaks at the sight of so much care and concern for my little girl. My Ruthie. Tears fill my eyes as the reporter begins her segment, the camera roving the crowd.

"I'm Rachel Monroe with Channel Three news, bringing you breaking news. I am standing outside the home of a local Tacoma resident, where last night at approximately six p.m., eight-year-old Ruth West was abducted from her yard. She left her home to take out the trash and never returned. Local law enforcement have been scouring the vicinity since the abduction was reported, and they have yet to find a substantive lead. Here with me now is the victim's mother, Gray West, with a plea to our viewers to call in suspicious activity or disturbances in the neighborhood. Gray, what would you like say?"

Rachel moves the mic toward me, and I speak from the heart, just as Fillippe told me to do.

"We're worried sick, her brother, sister, and me, and pray that Ruthie will be home soon. Ruthie is a fighter, and I know she'd never give up, so we won't either. If you know anything about where she might be, please, call the police. Help me get my baby back." I wipe away the tears that fall down my cheeks and finish the interview, glad Fillippe suggested I do it. If there is anything I can do to help the search, I will.

. . .

Afterward, I ask Callahan if I can be taken to the mobile command post and she nods. "Actually, I'm headed there now."

I turn to the kids. "Abel, can you stay here with Olive? You can meet her friends."

"Of course, Mom."

Walking down the street with Callahan, we march over the accumulating snow. It's still falling, making me wonder what sorts of clues can be wrung out of the storm.

"You did great with the interview."

"I hope it helps somehow. I'm barely hanging on right now."

She clears her throat. "I want you to know I shared the audio file from our earlier interview with the team."

"Everyone?"

"It's in the official case file. That way, the officers on the other side of the state can access it too. Might help them there."

"Of course." I sigh. "I told you more about myself than I think I've told anyone in a whole year. Now, of course, lots of people will know about my past, but I will always remember that conversation in the kitchen. And if you were judging me the whole time, you didn't let it show. So thanks for that."

The mobile command post is a few yards

ahead, a large RV type of vehicle where officers are coming and going.

"I know you've been through a lot," Charlie Callahan says. "But what you said back there in the interview about Ruthie being a fighter? I have a feeling that your daughter gets that from you."

I smile somehow, despite the agony I'm facing. I look up to the sky, snowflakes in a flurry around me, and find myself praying to a God I don't pretend to understand.

I pray that Ruthie doesn't give up her fight anytime soon.

8

I'M STOPPED on the street by a woman I faintly recognize.

"Sorry, excuse me," she says, the sun rising behind her. "I'm Soria Scott, the dean of students at Ruthie's school."

"Oh, Tomas's mother," I say. Callahan nods, telling me it's perfectly fine to stand here and have a conversation. I appreciate having the officer with me because I feel so out of sorts, like I am floating above reality, and her presence grounds me.

Soria smiles weakly. "Yes, I am. I saw the eleven o'clock news last night; there was an alert of Ruthie's abduction. Tomas and I both wanted to be here this morning. He cares so much for Olive, and of course, we all care so much for Ruthie."

"Thank you," I say, the white snow blazingly bright, covering any clues. "I know Olive was grateful to see a familiar face this morning."

"Dozens of teachers and school district employees are helping with the ground search," Soria says. "I want you to know we will continue to do everything within our power to help."

Callahan introduces herself. "I heard you were working with Officer York earlier, providing school documents to the department?"

Soria nods. "Yes, it makes sense that anyone who is close to Ruthie might have information that could help."

"Can you think of anyone who might be ... might have ..." My words fall flat. What am I trying to suggest? That someone who works at the school Ruthie attends could have kidnapped her?

But why is it so impossible to think? I've pointed fingers at both Ruthie's brother and father. Why not the school bus driver or the lunch lady? At this point I can't rule out anyone. After all, after the week I've had, nothing should shock me. Patrick and Anna were murdered by their boss. Anyone is capable of doing any number of irreversible things. Sane people break; unhinged people crack; there are no guarantees that the people you trust should have your confidence.

It's a terrifying thought. Because if my world is all gray, if the black and white—the right and wrong—are truly washed away, then how can I ever trust anyone, really?

"I won't keep you. I just wanted to let you know we are here for you," Soria says, her eyes watery, and I know why. She is a mother, just like me. Her world could crash at any moment, same as mine. She has a mother's heart, which is a contradiction in and of itself. Both a fragile, breakable thing and a heavy weight that is unmovable.

We walk away, and Callahan asks if I'm okay.

I look over at her, realizing I know nothing about her. A woman who is clearly capable in a multitude of ways. "Do you have children?"

She shakes her head. "No. But I have a cat named Clarice."

"Why did you become a police officer?" I

ask, wanting to fight the cold with words as we walk over a bank of snow.

"When I was twenty, my boyfriend was buying me ice cream at a gas station. I was pregnant and craving it so bad." She looks over at me, giving me a smile even though I already know this story doesn't end well. "He had a pint of rocky road in his hand, and a man came in to rob the joint, shot him in cold blood."

"Oh my God," I gasp, grabbing her arm in shock.

"I lost the baby the next week, and just like that, my whole world, all my hopes and everything, were gone."

"I'm so sorry, Charlie."

She lifts her shoulders. "This is not a day for me to be talking about myself."

"I asked."

"I became a cop because I was angry, but I realized my heart had to be soft if I was ever gonna fight for justice." She looks at me. "So now some people think I'm a bit of a softy, but that's okay. I'd rather be soft than so hard I can't break."

I blink away the tears in my eyes, coming to the realization that every woman everywhere is fighting her own demons, her own doubts. Looking for a flicker of light to hold on to when the world seems more dark than dim. Looking for meaning in this mess.

"Thank you," I say. "For being here with me."

She juts out her chin. "I'm not the only one here for you." Up ahead, Boone stands, in his green winter parka, his black leather boots. Looking more like a man made for the mountains than a detective fighting crime in a crowded city.

Boone waves as I approach the mobile unit. He stands with other officers, and my eyes dart away from his, instead falling on Officer Truce. If Boone heard the recording I made in the kitchen, earlier this morning, then he knows more about me now than I have shared in the past and I can't help but wonder if that changes our friendship. Truth is, we haven't known one another long, yet I would be lying if I said his opinion of me doesn't matter. Because it does.

"What's the update, Truce?" Callahan asks, cutting to the chase, crossing over my insecurities because she doesn't know about them. Being around a group of highly educated and qualified adults reminds me of all my inadequacies. My lack of education or any formal training whatsoever. I am capable of alphabetizing books, placing them on shelves. I'm a library clerk, paid minimum wage, and while I am appreciative of my job, I know anyone with a grasp of the English language could do it.

I spent twenty years of my life at Garden Temple, living alongside a group of followers that grew ever so slowly. My aunt and uncle were some of the first to join up with Jeremiah after hearing him preach at their local church. Over time, they became two of one hundred and fifty disciples. And in all that time, there was never once a teacher on the compound with a degree in education.

The men on the compound had a construction company, and they would build houses and other projects. Everyone who joined donated their retirement funds and life savings—and there were two families who came right I after I moved in that had hefty inheritances that floated us for over a decade.

All that to say, when I stand among a group of highly trained individuals, I can't help but consider how they must see me. It is on my mind even at a desperate time such as this. Maybe more so, now that they can begin piecing together my story with my age—the reality that I gave birth to Abel when I was just fifteen. The implications that come with that are many. I don't have a high school diploma; my life story isn't something anyone would envy.

Truce clears his throat and begins to explain where they are with the ground search. His words keep me in the present, as does the cold that begins to sink into my bones. The weather is icy, twenty-eight degrees: an unprecedented cold spell in a normally mild climate. It's hard not to feel grim about the reality that my little girl might be out in the elements.

"The fact is we haven't found a single lead since the scarf. We are waiting for word over in Grant County to see if the interviews there might bring us closer to finding Ruth, but as of now, there is nothing definitive."

His words bite at my heart, and I draw in a deep breath, knowing my body is going numb, not because of the temperature but because of Truce's direct statement.

No one has any idea where Ruthie is.

"The neighborhood has been divided into a grid, and it's been scoured twice, by two different search groups. You have some incredibly devoted neighbors, Gray. Bart Tomkins has been leading a group, and so has Granger Coyer. If the snow starts melting, it will help. Clues could be buried."

I look back up to the sky, clear blue, and I hold out hope that maybe the sun will shine brightly. "It's not even seven a.m.," I say. "The snow could start melting soon. We could find something …" I start to shake, fear cutting deeper than the cold. "We have to find her," I say. "We have to—"

"We know," Boone says. "And we have some more possibilities."

"What?" I ask.

Boone looks over at Truce. "We will let you know as soon as we have something substantial to share. Until then, we want to mitigate gossip."

"Have you been going door to door?" I ask, ready to march up on porches if they haven't, rap my knuckles against wood doorframes and beg for some sort of mercy.

"Yes, we've canvasing the neighborhood, and will make another round in a few hours, stopping at homes that were empty earlier. Of course, the weather plays a big role in everything at the moment," Truce says. "And we have your home security footage at the police department."

"Good, because then there will be no doubt of when I came and left," I say, hating the idea of any suspicion that might be planted in someone's mind that I had a role in Ruthie's disappearance. "What can I do now? I feel like we're at a dead end."

"That isn't true," Truce says, but his tone doesn't convince me, and when neither Boone nor Callahan jump in with assurances, I'm left wondering if my worst fears are coming true. If my daughter is never coming back.

9

Boone offers to walk me back to the house and so, side by side, we start the trek down the familiar street. I feel everyone looking at me, peering through windows, pausing, and giving me sad waves of support. I appreciate it, but I just want a moment to think, without anyone staring.

Thankfully, Boone doesn't say a word, and it's like he knows the last thing I want to do right now is be overheard. I want to talk to him, but privately.

My eyes can't help but take in every detail in the neighborhood. The bushes that seem to be moving—only it's a cat looking for a hiding spot. A shriek that causes me to jerk back—only to see a child throwing a snowball at a friend. Everything has me on high alert. I can't afford to miss any detail right now. It might mean the difference between life and death for my little girl.

Once inside the house, I peel off my layers, grateful the heat is cranked up, and turn to find Boone doing the same thing.

"Everyone must be out looking," I say. The house is quiet.

"And Olive and Abel, you know where they are?"

I pull out my phone, showing him the text I got from Luna. "They both went over to her house. She lives in the black house with the pink porch two doors down. Which is good, she has kids their ages."

"You trust her?"

I nod. "I do."

Still, he pulls out his phone and makes a call. "Truce? Yeah, I need you to go to the pink porch house and do a walk through. I think they will cooperate. Yeah, I'm here with her now."

He shoves the phone back in his pocket. "York is on his way to Grant County. We sent him and another officer after Jeremiah was brought in this morning."

"Was he cooperative?" I ask, trying to

picture Jeremiah willingly doing what a police officer asked of him.

"Sounds like it. He is in holding, waiting for York to interview him."

"Can officers search his house now?"

Boone shakes his head. "No, they don't have the intimate knowledge that the Tacoma PD has. It's not how jurisdictions work."

"Even in a kidnapping?"

Boone nods. "We will call in the FBI if there isn't movement on the case in the next few hours. We passed the twelve-hour benchmark, and this is when things will hopefully ramp up. We have some leads, Gray. All hope is not lost."

I nod, gripping the back of the sofa, the information overload making me light headed. "I need to sit."

"You've got to take it easy. Do you need to lie down?"

I scoff at his suggestion. "I can't sleep. I'm on edge. Like I could lose my mind any moment. I just keep picturing someone taking her. Someone scaring her ... who would do that? If not Jeremiah, then who? She's just a child." I start crying then, harder than I have all morning.

Boone wraps me in his arms. "Hey, hey,

it's okay, Gray," he tries to soothe. "It's gonna be okay."

"Is it?" I ask, stepping back. "How? I'll never be okay if I lose my baby."

His eyes turn dark, and I know he understands my fear. He lost his daughter. He knows this pain, this suffering. Not in the same way, but in a way that is much too close for comfort. "If Ruthie is with Jeremiah, then I at least we know she is alive. If she isn't …" My sentence falls apart because there is no easy way to end it, and Boone doesn't pretend to know what to say.

Instead, he asks if I'm hungry. "I'll make you something to eat. Seems right considering you cooked for me a few times last week."

"I can't eat." I press my fingertips to my temples. "But I'll drink coffee. I need to stay alert."

"All right, we'll start with coffee," he says, walking to the kitchen. The pot is full, and I see someone dropped off more food. There are breakfast sandwiches and croissants on the counter.

I sit on a stool, my phone set out in front of me with the hope of a call telling me Ruthie has been found.

Boone hands me a mug. "Do you want to talk?"

I swallow, looking up at him. "Did you hear what I told Charlie earlier? I know she sent the audio file in for evidence."

"Of course I heard," he says. "Right after, I went over to Larchmont Motel and had a chat with your guy."

"Tony?"

He nods. "Yeah, he was scared shitless. A junkie terrified of getting caught."

"He wouldn't hurt anyone," I say. "He means well."

Boone's jaw tenses. "He had XX grams of meth on him."

"He's a survivor. Not a criminal."

Boone drinks his coffee, and I know it's to avoid arguing with me.

"I met him when we first came into town," I explain. "I stayed there with the girls for a few weeks until I found an apartment that would rent month to month. He helped me out. A lot, actually."

"I'm glad to hear that." Boone sets down his coffee. "Because it sounds like you'd been through a hell of a lot before you got to Tacoma."

I bite my bottom lip. "I wanted to tell you

more, about my past, but it's complicated, Boone. More than complicated. And …" I look up at the ceiling, my hands wrapped around the mug, my heart pounding for all the things I want to say. "I know we just met, but I want you to respect me. And I'm scared that if you know everything, you never will."

Boone walks over and sits on the kitchen stool next to mine. Our shoulders brush and I'm relieved. It's easier not looking in his green eyes. It's easier not trying to decipher every emotion that passes over his face.

"Why do you care so much about my respect, Gray?"

"I've never had a man's respect before," I tell him plainly. "Certainly not Jeremiah's, not my uncle's, who took me in when I was ten. Not even Patrick's. I thought he was my friend, and he was using me to cover his own crimes." I exhale, reaching for a croissant and breaking it in half. "I suppose my father respected me. But that was so long ago, it's hard to remember."

"How long?"

"I was ten when my parents were killed in a car crash. I was with them. After, I was placed with my aunt and uncle, who were my guardians. They lived in Moses Lake."

"That's where you met your children's father, Jeremiah?"

I press a hand to my cheek, tears in my eyes, my elbow resting on the counter. Boone turns his head and looks at me. Our noses inches apart. I hoped sitting on stools would make this conversation easier, being side by side instead of face-to-face. I was ridiculously wrong. Now, he is closer than he has ever been. And in this moment, I will him to not look away. Because I want this man to see me. To know me. I want more than his respect.

"What?" he asks, his voice a whisper, gravelly and low and cutting deep into my heart. His *what* is permission to trust myself. To trust myself with him.

"I feel like when you look at me, you see the girl I wanted to be before my parents died," I admit. "The girl who loved fresh flowers and holidays and family trips. The girl who planned on a life so much bigger than the one she got."

"And what do you see, Gray? When you look at yourself?"

The question surprises me. And I feel my shoulders shake. The tears fall freely, and his hand reaches for mine. He grips it tight. In an *I won't let go* way.

“I see a woman who was given to a man when she was only fourteen,” I tell him. “As his bride. I see a woman who waited too long to leave a life that held her captive. I see a woman who fought for a chance at happiness only to watch it slip away. Ruthie is gone, and how could I let that happen, Boone? How could I be so weak, so stupid? I want your respect, but I know I’ll never have it because how could a man like you ever respect a woman like me?”

Boone’s eyes are glassy, and he won’t let me look away. “Dammit, Gray. Don’t do that. Don’t put yourself in a corner. You told me you gave yourself the name Gray because the world isn’t black and white. Well, hell, my name’s Orion—a constellation that fills the night sky. And you know what? I’ve spent time looking up, trying to find answers in the great beyond, praying for meaning to come out of this mess we call life. And you know what I found?”

“What?” I ask, knowing he lost his little girl to cancer, believing if he’s learned a lesson, it’s worth hearing. “What did you find?”

“That we can’t spend our days wishing things had gone differently. Because if we do that, then we miss out on what our life actually is. And what your life is, Gray, is goddamn glorious. You're not weak, and you're not small. You are a mother fighting for her child, and that's the fiercest thing on earth. I know that because I watched my ex-wife fight for her little girl. And I know what sort of strength that takes. You want my respect? Good. Because you have it." He wipes his brow with the back of his hand. "We *will* find Ruthie. And after that, we're gonna deal with the son of a bitch who made you believe all these lies."

10

Charlie Callahan enters the house, and upon seeing Boone and I close to one another in the kitchen, she clears her throat. "Am I interrupting something?" she asks.

Boone pulls back, coughing in his hand. "No," he says, his eyes still on mine. "I need to read through the information collected on Cory Jacobson."

"Is that something to be discussing here?" Callahan asks.

Boone reaches for his winter parka, pulling it on. "You wanna hold things back from Gray, I won't stop you. I'm just doing what I think is right."

Callahan snorts. "The men in this department think they can do whatever they want."

I lift my eyebrows, not expecting them to be divided. I thought Charlie was being direct with me, but maybe she knows things and *is* holding back.

"What aren't you saying?" I ask her.

"Nothing." She gives Boone a hard look as he heads to the front door.

Boone turns to me. "I'll come by later with an update."

"I'm her appointed liaison," Callahan interjects. "You sure you aren't too close to this case, Boone?"

He smirks. "I'm sure."

After he leaves, I ask her what that was all about.

"If a female officer was getting cozy with the parent of an abducted child it would be an issue. But Boone seems to be able to do whatever he wants."

"You think he shouldn't be working to find Ruthie?"

Callahan pulls out her tablet and sits on the couch. I walk over to her and sit down beside her. "I'm saying it's good to have an unbiased opinion when it comes to the law, to justice."

"Boone is just trying to help. And I trust him."

"I'm glad to hear that. I don't have anything against him; It's just I was friends with Taylor."

"His ex-wife?"

Charlie nods. "We went to the academy together."

"She's a police officer too?"

Charlie nods. "She moved to the Seattle Police Department after losing Suzannah."

"Please don't ask someone to take him off the case," I say, my words soft but urgent. "I need him here."

Charlie exhales. "I know you do," she says. "And I'm not planning on stirring up trouble for you. If there's anyone who can help find your little girl, it's him."

I pull out my phone and scroll through the texts from my neighbors and coworkers at the library. My eyes heavy as I read the messages of support.

I open the group chat and type a message.

Me: ***Thanks everyone for your support. There is no update yet. Every minute counts and we're just hoping for some lead.***

Julia: ***Is there anything you need?***

Me: ***You are all already doing so much.***

Luna: ***Abel and Olive are here drinking hot cocoa. My heart is just breaking for you all.***

Kendall: ***We're praying for sweet Ruthie. <3***

Kendall may be someone new in my life, but she turned around from her weekend away to help with the search. Tears fall down my cheeks. The hardest part of leaving Garden Temple was walking away from my sister wives. They were my support system even if we didn't always see eye to eye. I feared I would never have female companionship again, but this neighborhood has welcomed me and my children with open arms. And even though I am faced with a crisis so dark and terrible, another part of me still holds on to hope that the world isn't just an awful place. That it is also filled with good people with pure intentions.

I check the weather, relieved to see the temperature is already rising, that the snow has stopped. My eyes are heavy, and I tell myself to focus, to respond to the texts, but it's hard to concentrate when my mind is running to so many places, so fast.

The front door opens and my body jerks awake. I fell asleep with my phone in my hand and immediately jump up, scared I missed something. I glare at Callahan who is typing notes on her tablet. "Why did you let me fall asleep?"

"It's only been an hour, Gray. You needed rest."

"Mom?" Olive's voice cuts through my anger at Charlie for letting me sleep.

"Oh honey," I say, standing, moving toward her and Abel as they come in through the front door.

"Is there any news?" Olive asks.

I shake my head. "Nothing yet." Her shoulders fall, and she runs her hands over her face. "You okay?" I pull her in for a hug.

"Not really," she says, and her shoulders begin to shake, the tears I know she's been holding back finally falling. "I'm so scared, Mom."

"I know, sweetie. I know." I hold her close, looking over her shoulder at Abel. He rubs his eyes, clearly torn up too. Neither of them slept much last night, and I'm sure the stress is beginning to eat away at them.

"How was it at Luna's?" I ask.

"Weird," Olive says, wiping her eyes.

"I'm glad you're back home."

Callahan tucks her tablet into her messenger bag. "I'm going to get something to eat." She walks toward the kitchen.

"Has she been here the whole time?" Abel asks.

"She was assigned to me from the police department. It's nice, actually. If she hears anything, I'll be the first to know."

"I heard Boone went over to Cory's house," Olive says. "Did she tell you that?"

I frown. "No, but maybe they are trying to protect us in case ... in case something goes sideways."

"Aren't you going crazy though?" Abel asks, his hands balled into fists. His anger is growing, and I feel it as he speaks, his voice fraught with urgency. "Feeling like you aren't doing anything?"

"They said we can't help with the ground search, Abel. That we need to stay put."

I feel his frustration though. It's like we are sitting ducks, doing nothing while Ruthie is gone.

"Did you speak with Bethany again?" I ask.

Abel shakes his head. "No, not since this morning."

"Can we call again, for an update?"

"She isn't answering her phone. I'm guessing Lydia took it."

Callahan is heating up something in the microwave, and my stomach rolls. I've only had a bite of a donut and too much coffee.

"I'm hungry," Olive says as if reading my mind. "Is it bad to be hungry not knowing if Ruthie ... if ..."

"No," I promise. "We need to be strong for her."

In the hour I slept, there has been a food delivery. Callahan is helping herself to enchiladas and I'm glad. I don't want her leaving to get food. I feel safer having her here.

"Why is Boone at that guy Cory's house?" Abel asks Callahan as I dish up plates of the cheesy tortillas.

"They're hoping to get a better picture of who Cory is," Callahan says, matter-of-factly.

"Is 'better picture' code for something?" Abel presses.

Callahan shakes her head. "No, and I'm not spying on you or trying to hide something either. The ground search is underway, and until we have a suspect, or a clue to go on, we have to be patient."

"Patience won't get Ruthie back," Abel grunts, grabbing a fork.

"I know you're angry," she continues. "But don't be mad at me. I'm trying to help."

"And we are so grateful for that," I say. "I just think we are all on edge."

"Abel met Sophie and her friends," Olive

says, wanting to diffuse the intensity of the room. I could squeeze her in gratitude. "Her friends were over, making spaghetti for the volunteers."

"That's nice," I say. "What did you think of them?" I ask Abel.

"I think they are all lost souls." Abel eats at the table, not adding more. Olive looks at me and shrugs. I notice Callahan take in a sharp breath, and it makes me protective of Abel, of his innocence. He only knows what he has been taught. And all he has learned from his father is a bunch of lies.

"Sophie was talking about Cory," Olive adds, eating the enchiladas on her plate. I eat too, quickly, feeling guilty at the idea of enjoying a meal when my daughter is gone.

"What about him?"

"She said he has friends who have all dropped out of high school. And that he leaves the house late at night."

"Well, Boone is talking to him now," I tell her, thinking Cory sounds like a teenager, not a kidnapper. "So we'll know soon enough if he has something to do with Ruthie."

After everyone eats, I wash the lunch dishes, wanting something to do with my hands. Through the kitchen-sink window, I see the sky turn gray, and rain begins to pour. Relief floods through me. If the snow turns to slush, it will be easier to find a clue.

"It's coming down hard," Callahan says. "I bet the officers at the mobile unit are getting rained out."

The back door swings open, and it's Boone and Truce, both scowling. Both drenched.

"God," Truce groans, pulling down the hood of his winter coat. "That was unexpected."

"Guess it's a good thing for the temperature to rise," Boone says. "But it's gonna mean people out searching are gonna be taking a break until the rain stops."

"Did you talk to Cory?"

"Hardly," Boone grunts. "That kid refused to talk. His grandma was no better."

"What do you mean?" I ask.

Callahan lifts her eyebrows but doesn't tell Boone to course correct. She wants to know what Cory and his grandma said just as badly.

"She was extremely uncooperative. Let us inside, but had no idea what we were there for. Cory showed up at the house midway through the conversation and basically cussed us out for asking questions. That kid has a temper."

"What happens next?" Abel asks.

"We get a search warrant. Won't be difficult. He has no alibi for the time Ruthie was taken, refuses to answer questions, plus Sophia, the neighbor, has made a statement about his voyeurism. Once we have the warrant, we'll go back and search the house."

"When?" I ask.

"Soon," Boone says. "Very soon. And I promise, Gray, we won't stop until we find her." But he shares a look with Charlie that makes my skin crawl. A teenage boy who kidnaps a child and isn't looking for ransom has only one intention—and it is more twisted than I am prepared to face.

11

KNOWING that a shower made me feel better, I urge Abel and Olive to take turns doing the same. They agree, though I know they find it difficult to leave me alone after a morning at Luna's. They're anxious for answers. So am I.

Of course, we're hoping the search warrant for Cory's house will lead to something, but I think the three of us are on edge —too on edge—to be that hopeful, to believe it's that easy.

Truce approaches while the kids are upstairs, and I offer him coffee, but he refuses. "We have a lead, Gray. The surveillance camera from your front porch revealed a suspicious vehicle."

"Suspicious?" I remember the Town Cars

that had circled my block a few weeks earlier. Now I know it was the drug dealers that Patrick had been working with, wanting payment for their product or the product itself. I didn't know that at the time and was horrified to learn I'd been peddling drugs for my friend. I thought I was simply being watched by Jeremiah, but that wasn't the case at all.

As far as I know, Jeremiah still didn't know where I lived at that time. Of course, maybe now he does. Maybe he came here last night, angry at Abel for leaving, and took Ruthie to spite me.

Lydia's words from our conversation earlier still ring through my ears. *"Ruthie is always here. In spirit, sister. As are you."* The words felt eerie even as she said them, and as I think about them now with Truce in front of me, the chilling effect hasn't evaporated.

Truce runs a hand over his jaw, removing his hat. He sits down on the couch, and I sit opposite him in an armchair. Callahan is still here too. Her tablet's in her hand; she's taking notes—she takes notes on everything. Charlie Callahan is a strong woman. While I don't particularly like the fact she tried to put Boone in his place, I do appreciate her no-nonsense approach to this case. To me.

I spent so many years cowering behind men in the shadows, nodding my head politely and listening obediently, allowing my husband to make decisions for my life, and our children's lives, decisions that I didn't necessarily agree with but didn't have the wherewithal to object to.

Charlie Callahan is not like me. She is confident and strong, and she's not taking anybody's bullshit.

Whenever we get to the other side of this mess, and have both Ruthie home and Bethany safe, I'll do whatever it takes to become a woman like Charlie. It's not that I want to forget who I am, but I want to grow, evolve, be a better version of myself, the kind of woman who doesn't allow everyone else to take the driver's seat.

Of course, Boone has told me I'm wrong to doubt myself so much. He says he respects me. Thinks I'm a fighter, a survivor. I want to believe him, but right now I'm not ready to. The guilt of Ruthie being taken gnaws at me. What kind of mother am I?

"Do you have an update on Jeremiah?" I ask. "Was it his car?"

"We don't have word from Grant County yet," Truce tells me. "I'm still waiting to hear from York about the interview. I'm hoping to any minute now. It's been a long day for everyone, and I know you're included in that. I wish we had Ruthie back here already."

I nod, eager to hear more. "So whose car is it? Was it here today?"

"Not today, which is even more reason to look into this, but for the two days prior to the abduction, there was a car that circled your block several times, stopping directly across the street. Did you notice this activity?"

I shake my head. "No, I didn't. But I had so much going on with Patrick and Anna.

"Right, Anna." Officer Truce clenches his jaw. "Tell me what you know about Anna's husband, Jasper Treble."

"Jasper?" I say, thinking back to a handful of days ago when we were at the wELLEness Center, Elle standing up in front of her team, offering her condolences for the losses of her colleagues and trying to pep us up with a new product line. Jasper was there, grieving the wife he had just learned had died, been killed, murdered. He broke down crying, sobbing, really, shoulders shaking. I'd never seen a grown man so broken. It had stunned me then. It stuns me now.

"Why are we talking about Jasper?" I ask.

"Jasper's car is the one that had been circling and stopping in front of your house. Watching you."

"Are you sure?" I say. "That doesn't make any sense. Anna had just died."

"Exactly. Anna had just died, and he was here at your house, watching you for hours."

"You're sure it was him?" I ask. "I've hardly ever talked to him. I'd been to his house a handful of times, of course, with the girls, but ..."

"With the girls?" Truce pinpoints. "So he knew Ruthie."

"Yeah, Jasper knew Ruthie. But ..."

"No. There's no room for buts right now, Gray. Right now, we are looking for evidence, things to go on."

"You think Jasper might have, might have ..." The words catch in my throat, too ridiculous to entertain. "You think Jasper might have taken Ruthie?"

"Right now, the idea of ruling out a suspect before we have a better idea of their involvement is out of the question. I'm going over to Jasper's to interview him right now, but I wanted information from you first."

"What kind of information?" I ask.

"How was he with Ruthie? How well did he know her? Was he interested in her?"

"Interested?" I say. I lick my lips, trying to think. "No. I mean, he was nice enough to her, would play catch in the backyard or get her a second helping of food if we were over for dinner. But Anna and Jasper didn't have children, and Anna's gone now. It doesn't make sense."

"How badly did he want children?" Truce asks.

I exhale, thinking. "I know Anna was adamant about not having them. She had her own plans and visions for her life." My words fall short, thinking how all those plans died too quickly, laid to rest just like her. Was Jasper desperate for a child after Anna refused to give him one? Would that be motivation enough to come take my little girl?

"Let me explain why we're looking at him."

I hold up a hand. "I get why you're looking at him," I say, looking over at Charlie Callahan, whose eyebrows raise again, the smallest hint of a smile on her lips as I stick up for myself. "I understand perfectly well what you're saying, Officer Truce. You think Jasper might have taken Ruthie, and you have reason to believe he had motive to do so. He was a grieving man, clearly upset, and wanted a little girl. He was angry at me for my involvement in the first place, even though I did nothing to get Anna killed."

"Okay," Truce says, hands raised in defeat. "I was wrong to suggest you didn't understand. Clearly, you have a good grasp on the situation. I'm just letting you know Jasper is a suspect. You need to stay at home and not mention this to anyone until we have more answers. If there is *anything* you remember, anything at all about Jasper that you think could help us, please let me know. Disclosing even the smallest recollection can help us move forward."

I wish I had more to say. I wish I had stories of Jasper looking at Ruthie a beat too long, memories of Jasper's eyes filled with desperation for a little girl. But I don't. I simply remember Anna didn't want children and her husband did. I remember his shoulders shaking at the wELLEness Center, missing his wife. At least I thought it was because he missed her. Did he? Or was he glad she was gone? Truth is, I don't know Jasper any better than I know anyone in this room. I am surrounded by people I've just met, and I don't have the intuition it takes to rule people out.

"Truce," Callahan says. "If Gray remembers more, I'll let you know. I'll keep a close eye on her. She's not going anywhere. She's not talking to anyone. Go. Interview this guy. At this point, we need a lead. We need a suspect that's viable."

"You don't think Jeremiah's viable?" I ask. Callahan and Truce share a look, and I know they know things about Jeremiah that I don't. "What?" I say. "Tell me something, please. I'm in the dark here."

"You're not in the dark, but Boone's on his way over," Truce says, exhaustion in his voice. "I think it's best if he's the one to tell you."

12

After Truce leaves, I pace the living room, looking out the large window. Outside on the street, there are cars lined up and people huddled in groups. The search parties have been out looking all morning and now it's getting late. Now they have completed their grids, looking for clues, and haven't found anything.

Callahan clears her throat. "The search parties are going to go back out. They're hoping now that the snow has begun to melt, they might find something."

Find something that would lead them to my daughter, to my Ruthie. A clue that might help them discover where she was taken and why.

Upstairs I hear Abel and Olive arguing. I run a hand over the base of my neck, tense from head to toe.

"I wish that they would stop," I say.

Callahan nods, understanding. "Everybody deals with their stressors differently," she says.

"Ain't that the truth?" My voice is wry, but I agree with her. Some people drink to deal with their anxiety; some people smoke; some people lie, and some people cheat; some people sleep; some people work harder than they should, and some people cry and give up. Let Olive and Abel argue; let them relieve their anger at the situation. Stepping in now and telling them to push down their emotions seems the least helpful option.

I blink, anxious as I see Boone's car pull into my driveway. It's been over two hours since Truce left.

"He'll tell me everything, right?" I ask.

"Yes," Callahan says. "He'll give you the full report that was given to him by York over in Grant County."

"Is it good news?" I ask.

Callahan presses her lips together. "What kind of news is good at this point?" she says.

Her words sting, but I tell myself Charlie

is a realist. Me? I'm not cut from the same cloth. I find myself wrapping the cardigan I'm wearing tighter around my body before pulling open the door, bracing myself for a miracle. It's possible, isn't it?

I stand on the front porch, watching as Boone gets out of his car, locks it, waves to another officer who's leading a group of people on to the search. The sky above is covered in clouds. Rain falls down on the slush that covers my front yard. The weather in Western Washington is unpredictable, often rainy, mostly mild, but then there are storms like this, sweeping in faster than anyone expected. Blanketing the city in snow, then rain, when what we really need is bright blue skies and sunshine, but we were not given that this February. Instead, we were given a snowstorm the same night my little girl was taken.

Boone nods in greeting. "How you holding up, Gray?" he asks.

"I've been better," I tell him honestly. "Much better."

"I know."

"Do you have news?" I ask. "News that can help?"

"Jeremiah doesn't have Ruthie," he says.

His words don't seem to penetrate my mind. I shake my head, not wanting to believe him. Ruthie being with her father would be the best-case scenario at this point.

"I have the report, and with Callahan here, I'd like to share it with you," Boone says.

"So York was able to interview Jeremiah?" I ask, wanting to find an error in the findings.

Boone nods, wiping his feet on the front mat as he walks inside. He unzips his coat and hangs it on a hook by the door, the raindrops falling to the hardwood floor like the tears that have splashed down my cheeks for nearly twenty-four hours. Too many hours.

"Your neighbor Granger has headed up a group going to the slope on the back end of the neighborhood. And Bart—I think he lives in the house with the pink porch—he's leading a group in the other direction. It's been a long day, but your neighbors are still here for you, Gray. Nobody's given up."

I nod, hearing him on that point but wanting to get back to Jeremiah. "I saw as much through the window, but I've been locked inside all day and am feeling so antsy," I tell him, not caring that Callahan is listening. "It's so painful to be inside when I want to be out there helping, doing something."

"I know. This must be excruciating, but it's better this way. Want to sit down so I can tell you what I know?"

I nod, wanting to get to the bottom of it, the end of it, knowing if Ruthie had been with Jeremiah, she would be here right now, or Boone would be smiling and telling me she's in transport back home.

But he's not, and she isn't, and we're here. The house feels cold. Before I sit, I walk to the thermostat and crank it up. Olive and Abel are upstairs, quiet now, and I can only hope they're telling one another stories about the lives that they've lived this last year apart. Filling in the blanks and connecting dots. I know Abel is stressed out and wanting to talk to Bethany.

I want to help him. Once we know what's happening with Jeremiah and the people at Garden Temple, we'll have a better picture of how to help the girl he loves.

I sit down as Boone pulls out his tablet. He flicks his finger across the screen and looks up at me.

"How can you be sure he doesn't have her?" I ask. "Did you search his house? He has a really big house and the compound is ..."

"I have been here this entire time, Gray. But if you're asking about the officers in Grant County and what they've done, they did a sweep of Jeremiah's house, and while you might have reason to believe he has connections with other people on that property, the warrant let us look inside Jeremiah's house and no further."

"What did you find?" I ask. "I mean, what did *they* find?"

"Jeremiah had an alibi and it checks out. He couldn't have been here."

"How do you know?" I say. "He's a liar. That's all he does. His whole life is built on lies. You know, before he started that compound and built it up, he was a construction worker? Yeah. He has all of those people eating out of the palm of his hand, believing he is something special, something holy. But he isn't. You need to arrest him, even if he doesn't have Ruthie. He's a bad man, Boone."

Boone gives me a hard look. "I want to know all about that. All about his followers or disciples or whatever you want to call them, but in this exact moment, Gray, you need to focus. You need to focus on your little girl. Getting caught up in the other messes this man has made will not help you. Your daughter is not with him. Do you understand me?" Boone speaks clearly, driving the point home. He doesn't know where my little girl is.

My hands are fists; my eyes are glassy; my heart pounds, and I want to scream. I want to yell. I want Ruthie to be with Jeremiah because then the questions would be answered. The problem would be solved, and my little girl would be coming home, and I hate that he doesn't have her. Not that I want her with him, but I want her back. And if she isn't there, that means we don't know where she is.

That means we don't know who has her, why they have her.

Maybe it's Jasper, Anna's husband, desperate for a daughter. Maybe it's Cory torturing her in his bedroom. I don't know. I just know that whatever the answer is, it's infinitely more complicated than I wanted it to be.

I want Ruthie to be safe. I want Ruthie to be home. And right now, I don't know if she is either. The tears are falling faster than I can catch them with my palm and wipe them away, and Callahan hands me a tissue.

I don't want the tissue. I want my little girl.

"I wanted her to be there," I cry. "Not that I want her to be with him, but I wanted to have this finished. All morning I've been hoping; I've been praying that she is okay. That she'll be home before bedtime, that I can tuck her in, and I can tell her I'll keep her safe. I've been hoping that it wasn't as awful as it could be. A stranger stealing her way into the night, taking her away forever—"

"We don't know that she's gone forever," Boone says, cutting me off.

And I know I'm hysterical, but maybe it's time for me to be hysterical. Maybe it's time for me to let go of any control that I've been trying to hold on to because what am I controlling now? What do I have now? Nothing but a dead end.

"You're sure she wasn't there?" I ask. "You're sure?"

Boone turns the tablet to face me. "Come here, sit down," he says and I do. Callahan sits beside him as well, the three of us on the couch leaning into the tablet that he holds in his big hands, and he presses play.

A video begins and it's a place I know. A voice I know. A sound I remember.

Jeremiah is on the pulpit. He is at the church that he built with his own two hands, that my uncle helped construct. That the men who believe Jeremiah is a prophet nailed into place. It's filled with people. Some I know, and some I've never seen before.

"You've all come to this service tonight," Jeremiah's voice booms through the video, "because the end is near. The time is now. The garden in which we have grown is ready to harvest."

There's cheering and clapping. I look down at the time stamp. I see how long there is left in the video, an hour. An hour of Jeremiah preaching and prophesizing, speaking in tongues and telling a story that has been given to him by the heavens—allegedly. As he speaks from the pulpit, he breaks into a sweat, his body convulses, and he grips the podium, bracing himself as he cries out about the word of God. How he has been called upon by God himself to deliver the message, to save his people, to bring them home. For a believer, it is proof of the power that Jeremiah has.

I've seen enough. Because I've seen it all, because I've heard it all. I close my eyes.

"That's him. His alibi is a church service." I shake my head, let down. "His congregation gathered around him," I say, "hanging on to every word he speaks."

"You've heard these sorts of things before?" Callahan asks. "This message?"

I nod. "Plenty of times. He had a revelation from God every other week. It's what kept people coming back. Kept people believing. If he had a direct line to God who was telling him their purpose, the plan, how could they not come back to listen? They were as desperate as he was." I feel nauseous. "I don't want to watch anymore," I say. "I can't."

Boone nods, turns off the screen. Then he silently hands it to Callahan, who takes it and walks into the kitchen. I hear the video begin again. She's pressed play. I don't know if she's hanging on to every last word Jeremiah speaks, but she's listening.

"I hate him," I say.

"I know," Boone says, "I hate him too."

"I wanted her to be there," I say. "I wanted her found."

"So did I," Boone tells me, and he takes my hand, and he squeezes it tight, and I hold on even tighter.

"I need to find her," I tell him. "The day is passing far too fast and I'm scared."

"I know," Boone says. "I know you're scared, but don't give in to that. Don't give in to your fears, Gray. Hold on to hope for that promise of your little girl coming back, being here again."

I wipe my eyes and I look at him. "Thank you," I say.

"For what?" he asks.

"For believing that we'll find her."

Boone nods. "We will," he says. "Gray, I promise you, we will."

13

Olive and Abel enter the kitchen freshly showered, their faces bright, their eyes red, and I know they've been crying all day, same as me. Still, I'm glad they're taking care of themselves.

"So did you find anything out?" Olive asks Boone.

I appreciate my twelve-year-old daughter's ability to speak up, to ask questions when she needs an answer. It's what I want for her. It's why we're here, why we left Garden Temple.

"I'm sorry, Olive, but the news isn't exactly what we hoped for," Boone tells her honestly.

"So what is it?" Abel asks, his voice harder, hoarse.

"Your dad didn't take Ruthie," I say. "Last night, he was holding a service at the church, so he couldn't have been in both places."

"Maybe someone else took her," Abel says. "Maybe there was another guy doing his dirty work."

"We have no reason to believe that is the case," Boone says. "He wasn't even aware that you had come to your mother's house," he says.

Abel frowns. "Does he know now? Did you tell him where I went?" Boone and Callahan share a glance. I hate their secrets. They're starting to bother me more than I'd like.

"Your father knows you're here, yes," he says.

"Why'd you go and do that?" Abel asks. He looks at me. "Mom, why did you let them blow my cover?"

"I didn't let anybody do anything," I say, "and first of all, I gave an interview this morning clearly showing where we were. But it's probably better that your father knows where you are, especially now. This is a big deal. Ruthie's gone," I say. "And I know you have issues with your dad. *I* have issues with your dad, but this isn't the time to argue about them. I don't care if Jeremiah knows where we are now. I'm glad he does. I'm glad I don't have to hide constantly, worried that he's going to come find me."

I'm shouting. I never shout, but I don't care.

"You know how long I was scared of your dad hurting me?" I ask my children. "I've been scared of your father since I was fourteen years old. I've been scared not just of him finding me, but of him touching me, of him using me, of him fighting me, of him threatening me. I'm done with it," I seethe. "I'm done letting Jeremiah have power over me. I'm done."

My children are stunned, and Boone and Callahan are too. And to be honest, I'm stunned myself. I never do this, lay it out there, put all my cards on the table. But I'm dead serious when I say I have nothing left to lose. Jeremiah doesn't have Ruthie. But somebody does. And I'm not going to stand here and be scared of the man who hurt me for so long when there are bigger things at stake.

"I'm done hiding from him. If he wants to come after me, he can. But he won't," I say. "He never cared about me. He never needed me. When I left a year ago, I thought he did. I was foolish enough to think that Jeremiah cared about what happened to me. But he's only ever cared about himself. My leaving gave him an opportunity to spin a story that his followers were begging to hear. He'd been scorned by the woman he took in as an orphan."

"Why did he marry you?" Abel asks.

My throat grows dry at that, and the room is so quiet I could hear a pin drop. But the pins all feel like they're stuck in me, burying themselves deeper.

"He married me to protect me. That's what he said. He really wanted a wife. He had been preaching that he was going to be celibate forever and never get married and that was God's will. But he was a man who was thirty. He wanted a wife."

Boone and Callahan might find this hard to believe that at fourteen I would end up with a man who was twice my age, but if they had been there, back then at Garden Temple, seeing the way everyone looked at Jeremiah, the way they still look at him now, they'd be able to understand there was an aura about him, a glow, a power. I wanted a taste of it. When he offered, I didn't even think to refuse.

"I was supposed to marry someone else," I explain, "but then that man died, and so Jeremiah took his place."

For a moment, I consider telling the whole truth, laying it out there—that I killed a man and Jeremiah knew. At the time it felt like protection, but later I realized it was a ruse to fulfill his own need. He married me, promising to keep my secret safe. But this is not the time to reveal all of the past. Now is the time to look at the present, to find Ruthie.

"Oh," Olive says. "I never knew why you and Dad ended up together."

I run a hand through my hair. "Yeah, well, it was a long time ago," I say. "And I hate him, but I am thankful for you both, and for Ruthie, and I wouldn't trade you for anything."

"You're glad all that happened to you?" Abel asks, doubtful. "When all is said and done?"

"I don't regret having you, if that's what you're asking. I'm glad I'm your mother. Being your mother is the privilege of my life, and I wouldn't trade it for anything."

Abel nods. "We'll find her, Mom."

"Will we?" I ask, my voice raw, my heart rate slowing, my breath shallow. A moment ago, I was ready to go down fighting. Now, the air has left me, and I feel empty, defeated. "I hope you're right," I say. "I hope we'll find her, but ..." There's a crackling on Boone's radio.

"Are you ready to go into the Jacobson house?" a voice asks Boone.

Boone replies, "Are you headed there now with the warrant?"

"Yep. On our way."

"I'll meet you there," Boone says. He looks at us. "I know you have a lot going on emotionally," he says, "but having a search warrant for Cory Jacobson's house is a good thing for this case, for Ruthie. Okay?" He speaks as if giving us a pep talk.

I nod, needing his affirmation. "You're going to go over there now?"

"Yes," he says. "I'm going to go over there, getting to the bottom of this, finding out if Cory is the creep we thought or if he's just a fucked-up kid. Excuse my language." Abel smiles.

"Okay, go," I say.

Olive takes my hand. "Don't worry, Boone. I'll stay with my mom. I'll make sure she's okay."

Boone smiles, tips his head, and leaves.

Callahan quietly walks out of the kitchen toward the living room, leaving us alone.

"There's more to that story, isn't there," Abel asks, "about you and Dad?"

I nod. "Yeah, there is. But it's not for today."

Abel nods, understanding. "So what happens next? I'm going crazy in this house."

I nod. "Me too. I'm pacing, walking in circles. All I want to do is get outside and try to find her, do something."

Olive smiles. "Well, then let's go."

"You want to go look for her?" Abel asks.

She nods. "I have to find my sister. I have to know I did all I could."

I twist my lips, listening as Callahan presses play on the tablet. I hear the recording of Jeremiah at the service. She's listening again. I frown. What is she hoping to hear? Before I can answer the question, I look at my kids.

"Okay," I say. "Let's go out the back door. We can do a search of our own."

14

WE EXIT the back door with our jackets pulled up high. We pull our hoods over our heads, but as I look up to the sky, the clouds have begun to part and though it's still gray, the rain isn't falling quite so heavily.

"Hopefully that will help with the investigation," I say.

"Probably better than the snow," Abel says. "I can only imagine how hard it was for people to look for clues when everything was covered."

We begin to walk with our heads down low, crossing through the backyards of our neighbor's houses, winding down the street. I don't want anyone to notice us, to stop us, and thankfully, no one does.

If anyone is trying to meet our gaze, we don't match it. Wordlessly, we head to the one place that is on all our minds—Cory's house. I know the police don't want us to be outside, but I feel claustrophobic inside. I need to be looking for my little girl, not staying locked inside my house. I've spent enough years feeling trapped.

When we're two houses away and can see it in the distance, Olive gets nervous. "Maybe we shouldn't be doing this. What if Ruthie is there, and we see something we can't unsee?"

Abel grunts. "Don't say that," he says. "Ruthie's fine. Ruthie is going to be perfectly fine. Maybe she got lost."

We all know how improbable that is. After twenty hours of her being gone, of course, it would be a happier ending to this story than the more likely one. The Jacobson house is on a corner lot. It's a big two-story Tudor, run-down and ramshackle, moss growing on a roof that needs to be replaced, and a crumbling red brick chimney. The front porch has a step with a cracked board, and the landscaping, though covered in snow and slush, has clearly not been tended to for years, maybe decades. The chain-link fence is ripped in places, and there's a big dog in the backyard growling. I hear him growling at anyone who passes.

Maybe Olive is right. Maybe being here is a bad idea. Still, I urge them on.

"I just need to know something," I tell them. "I'm tired of being the last to know."

"I don't know how much we'll find out being on the outside looking in," Olive says, her words making her sound so mature, so grown.

"I know," I say, "I just hope."

Hope, the word hangs in the air, and we watch as Boone and another officer I've never met before, speak with Cory's grandma on the front porch. She's in a wheelchair, an oxygen tank strapped to it, tubes running into her nose, helping her breathe.

Cory runs up the steps, his jeans long and dragging in the slush. He's in a black, short-sleeved T-shirt, not wearing a coat. His hair is long and greasy. He has a thick silver chain hanging from his belt loop holding his wallet in his back pocket.

"What the hell are you doing here?" he shouts at Boone and the other officer. "I said I don't know anything about this girl you're talking about. I have nothing to do with it," he says. "Why'd you come back here? Why don't you believe me?"

Boone hands him a piece of paper. I can't hear what he's saying because he's not shouting, but I'm guessing it's the search warrant.

"This is fucking bullshit," Cory shouts. "Grandma, you don't have to let him in. You don't have to do what they say."

She begins coughing loudly.

"Damn it!" Cory shouts. "She needs to get inside; why did you make her come out here? She's old; she's sick. She shouldn't be in the cold," he snarls. And he jumps up onto the porch, grabbing the back of the wheelchair and rolling his grandma back into the house.

Boone and the other officer follow, and there are four more officers standing in the yard. Neighbors are huddled in groups, but it's hard to make out who is who since everyone is scarfed up with beanies on their heads, winter coats keeping them warm.

Officers open the side gate, the chain-link fence rattling as they do, the dog growling and leaping at them. Olive jumps back, scared. She's never liked dogs like that, neither have I.

"They need to chain that thing up," Abel says. "It's going to bite someone." As if putting his words into action, an officer does just that, chaining the dog up to the fence and beginning a search.

"We're going to cover this yard," he shouts to the other officers. "We're going to start searching thoroughly. If you need to shovel snow, please do."

Everyone moves into action and we watch, craning our necks, not able to see the entire backyard. Boone is inside for what feels like ages. Eventually, all the officers in the backyard get called over to the back corner of the lot.

"I need forensics on the scene," an officer calls out, and someone jogs out to a patrol car and carries a case with him to the backyard.

I frown, wishing I had watched episodes of some criminal investigation show, but I don't know how this all works. I don't know who's being called in or for what. All I know is that if Cory has my little girl, I will make him pay. I will make him suffer. Ruthie is eight years old and does not deserve this. Any of this. She deserves a happy life, a warm bed, a roof over her head, a mother to tuck her in, not this.

Boone comes outside eventually and

walks around the back of the house. "What'd you find?"

It seems like ages before someone says something, does something, and I don't want to wait anymore. If they found something, I need to know what. I walk forward to the fenced yard, yanking the gate open, stepping into the muddy pit, the dog growling at me as I do. The officers turn, looking.

Abel and Olive are at my heels. "If Ruthie is here, we're here too. What did you find?" My voice is sharp, my eyes ablaze, my heart pounding, and my need so fierce, so, so fierce. My daughter is the only thing I have my vision set upon.

"You shouldn't be here," Boone says. "Gray, you're supposed to be at the house."

"I had to know. I had to find out. I needed to do something," I say, my voice shaking, my eyes darting. They land on an officer who is holding a plastic bag.

Inside there is a pink barrette, a butterfly.

"No," I say. "No." My voice cracks, and Abel wraps his arm around my shoulder. Olive takes my hand, squeezing it tight. My eyes meet Boone's. "No, that can't ... That can't be. She can't ... She can't be ..."

At the front of the house, Cory shouts, "I

didn't fucking have anything to do with this. I don't care what you found. I don't know where she is."

He's cuffed and being taken to a police car.

"That's Ruthie's hair clip," I say. "I watched her put it in her hair yesterday morning before I left for work."

Boone nods. "Okay. Okay, that's all we need to know."

"All you need to know?" I say. "Well, I need to know so much more than that. Where did Cory take her? What did he do to her?"

"Gray, listen to me. You need to get back to your house now."

"Oh, I need to get back to my house, is that it? While you just go on and find my daughter and ..."

"Yes," he says directly, "that's exactly what I mean. Abel, I need you to listen to me. It is time for you to take your mother home. Do you understand?"

Abel nods, taking in the gravity of the situation that clearly is going over my head. Cory has just been cuffed and taken into custody. The officers are wrapping crime scene tape around the chain-link fence.

The entire house is being swarmed by officers.

Abel drags me away. Boone's eyes lock on mine.

"Go home. I will call you. It's going to be okay."

I shake my head, frustrated. "Don't make promises you can't keep, Boone."

"I will do anything to find Ruthie, Gray. I know what it means to lose a child and ..." He runs a hand over his jaw, torn up. I am too. But I know what it means to lose a child too.

I lost Esther two days after she was born. And while that was fourteen years ago, it feels like yesterday. I know loss. I know pain. And I can't bear the idea of Ruthie out there in the world, alone, suffering too.

I swallow, collecting my thoughts. "Boone, if you make a promise you can't keep, it will make the fall that much harder."

"I'm not trying to make your life more difficult."

"I know you're not. But I'm so close to completely losing it, Boone. I'm scared."

"Go home. Talk to Callahan, okay? She's there. She's probably mad you're not. Go. I'm going to do my job now, Gray. Do you understand?"

I nod, shaking, trembling, knees buckling, trying to be brave in a way I've never been before.

I leave, letting my son guide me home. Tears streak my face as I catch the eyes of my neighbors. They see me now; they understand. A siren roars as it tears down my street away from the Jacobson house. Cory is cuffed in the back of that patrol car, and he'd better answer questions.

Kendall and Julia are huddled together, Luna with her husband, their hands covering their mouths, shocked and terrified. I'm shocked too. Luna comes over to me and gives me a hug. "What do you need?" she asks.

"I need to sit down," I tell her. "I feel shaky."

"Let's cross the street, okay?" Luna takes my hand and leads me to Julia's big front porch. There are rocking chairs lined up and I sit. Someone hands me a blanket, and I look out onto the street, feeling numb.

"I'm gonna head home and tell Charlie where you are, okay, Mom?" Abel says. He looks at my neighbors. "Don't let her out of your sight, okay? I'm taking Olive with me, okay?"

They walk back home, and I lean back in the chair. Julia brings me warm tea in a ceramic mug, and I wrap my hands around it. I'm grateful no one is asking me questions, thankful that I have their support. I watch the street as police cars arrive, then leave. As groups of volunteers congregate. As new reporters give updates to their camera crews. Hours pass; night falls; time is a blur.

"I think you should get home," Luna says. "Want me to walk you back?"

I stand, exhausted from nothing, heartbroken that an officer hasn't come to find me to give me an update.

Luna squeezes my hand as we stand on the sidewalk outside my house. "I'm a phone call away, all right?"

I walk to the front door, taking a deep breath as I pull it open. Callahan is in my living room, livid, but that's not all.

She's not the only person who is here. Standing next to Callahan is Jeremiah.

15

AFTER SPENDING SO MUCH of my life wrapped up in this man, it's strange how when I see him here, in my living room, it's as if I'm looking at a ghost. Someone who isn't even real.

He's tall and lean, handsome and discerning. He knows all the right things to say. My guard is up, up so high because I know his tricks. I know his games.

I won't let them work on me.

Callahan must have a few thoughts on Jeremiah herself. After all, she spent the last few hours watching and rewatching his preaching at Garden Temple. She knows his cadence, the way he can work a room.

Watching her watch him is an unnerving thing.

How many times has Jeremiah been in the same room as a woman who wasn't scared of him? He can probably count them on his hand. He has spent his life surrounding himself with people who worship him.

But Callahan comes from a different world. She didn't grow up in reverence with her head bowed. She is a woman who holds her head up high, who looks him in the eye.

"Gray, Jeremiah just arrived and asked to be invited in. Considering the weather, I let him in." She clears her throat. "Truce has called another patrolman in, and he'll be here any minute."

In the same moment, there's a knock on the door and I pull it open. The officer mentioned has arrived.

"You okay?" Callahan asks me.

"I needed some fresh air," I tell her. "I was just across the street."

"I take it you know what's going on?" Callahan asks pointedly. As my liaison, I'm sure the Tacoma Police Department has filled her in on everything that's going on.

Cory's been handcuffed and taken in a

police car. His house is considered a crime scene. Ruthie's barrette is in an evidence bag.

Will they find more inside that home? Terror winds itself up my spine. God, I hope not.

In all this time, I'm trying to collect myself, to wrap my mind around the fact that Jeremiah is here, standing in my home. His eyes fall on his children, Abel and Olive, the daughter he hasn't seen in a year.

"Jeremiah, what are you doing here?" I ask.

Olive starts crying. "Dad," she says, her voice betraying her, cracking under the weight of the emotion. I'm scared she's going to run to him. Wrap her arms around his waist. Cling to him.

Instead, she gathers herself. Wipes away her tears. "Did you do something to Ruthie?" she asks. "Did you hurt my sister?" Her voice is tight, taut, terrified.

"No," Jeremiah says. "I come in peace. I come with a broken heart. I come knowing your pain because I feel it too. I felt it for a year, Olive. Ever since you and your mother left home, I've been praying and searching. Desperate for you to come back, not knowing where to find you. And then as if by a miracle, a miracle of God, a police officer came to my home this morning and asked me questions about my little girl. The little girl I hadn't seen for so long because her mommy had stolen her away in the night, taken her from me. Olive," he says, kneeling down before her and taking her hand, "I've missed you, my child. Everyone has missed you so deeply."

"Stop it," I say. "Stop it, Jeremiah. Stand up."

He smiles slowly. "Oh, Grace, you always did like to put your foot down. Didn't you?"

"Why are you here?" I repeat.

"I'm here," Jeremiah says, "because I heard the horrible news that my little girl was kidnapped, and while this is terrible, I do believe God's providence will bring her back where she belongs, and likewise, will bring you all home. I think this is an act of God," he says. "I believe the Lord's will has made this happen as a punishment for your selfish choices of leaving the fold, of leaving your family."

"What are you saying?" I ask, my voice venomous, anger rising. "You think God's punishing Ruthie by having her abducted?"

"No," Jeremiah says sadly, shaking his

head. "I think God is punishing *you*, Grace, for leaving the only home you've ever known."

"Don't do this," Olive shouts. "Don't say that. It's not our home anymore. This is where we live, on this street. At 212 Pinecrest Point. This is where we live now, Dad. This is our home. Mom made it for us."

"Oh, child," Jeremiah says. "I know you must think such a thing. Your mother has put so many evil things in your mind because she is a broken woman who's turned away from her heavenly Father—"

"Dad," Abel cuts him off, "I think maybe this isn't the time for you to preach."

Jeremiah's eyes darken. "You think you can tell me what to do?" he asks. "After you left like that, scaring me and everyone else half to death? We didn't know where you had gone."

"I've done it before," Abel says, crossing his arms, shaking his head. "I've done it plenty of times. I knew where to go. I didn't ask you for permission because I don't need it."

"No?" Jeremiah asks. "What do you need, Son? What do you need, child?"

Abel steps forward, getting right up into

Jeremiah's face. "I need you to leave Mom the hell alone. And I need you to leave Bethany alone too. Go back to your compound and stop bothering us. Okay? We're busy looking for Ruthie."

Jeremiah shakes his head but doesn't raise his voice, not playing into this hand Abel wants to deal, not while Callahan is watching, not while another police officer is standing by taking notes, recording the audio, getting all the evidence he wants and needs.

Jeremiah won't say anything criminal. He knows better than to say anything that can get anyone in trouble because he knows how to work people. God knows he's worked me.

"I'm going to ask you each to calm down here," Callahan says. "Right now we are in the middle of a child abduction case, and the last thing we need is for family members to start falling out. All right? So I'm going to ask you, Gray, to go into the kitchen. Maybe make yourself something to eat. Get something to drink. A cup of coffee, maybe," Callahan says smartly. "I'm going to ask you to do that with Olive and Abel. And I am going to stay here with Jeremiah and Officer MacArthur. All right? That's what we're going to do right now. Our goal is to create an environment of peace so that we can focus on the task at hand. The task at hand is finding Ruthie, finding Ruthie safely."

"Well, good luck with that," Abel snaps. "If Cory has her, who knows what happened. I should go to the police station myself and let him know what I think of him."

Callahan's eyes whip up. "Abel, I know you're angry, but that line of thinking won't help anything. We're going to gather ourselves together and we're going to calm down. Do you understand? It's not the time to do something drastic."

The front door slams open. Boone has arrived. Callahan throws her arms up. "I was trying to calm everyone down, and this is your time to make a grand entrance?" she says, glaring at him.

I press my lips together. As much as I want to leave and do what Callahan asks, I know I can't.

Boone looks around the room. His eyes land on Jeremiah. He shakes his head. "I think it's time we had a little talk, don't you?"

16

I HAVE NEVER SEEN Jeremiah scared, but right now with Boone staring him down, I see fear in his eyes. There's a sort of vindication in it, in seeing the man who was my abuser for so long terrified. Maybe it's twisted, my desire to see the man who hurt me—who forced me to lie with his best friend for his sick game of power and control—scared.

There is admiration in the moment too, watching Boone step in, not speaking for me or on my behalf but offering me protection.

And not because he thinks I'm weak but because he understands how much I've already been through with this man, because he knows that Jeremiah is a dangerous person.

Sure, Jeremiah did not abduct our daughter, but he is here threatening us once again. He must have jumped in the car the moment the police released him in Grant County. He must have driven straight through, ending up here at my home to scare me, to scare Olive and to scare Abel.

What kind of father is he? Not a man like my own father.

My father was a dad. A dad who bought me popsicles in the summer and set up a sprinkler on warm sunny days, who remembered my birthday, who bought my mom flowers. I grew up with a dad. My children never have.

There's a difference between a father and a dad that suddenly feels vitally important to distinguish.

My heart aches for what my children have lost—a childhood full of happy memories, but also the the opportunity to have a dad who was their biggest fan, their number one ally, a person who could always be counted on to be in their corner.

All of that passes through my mind as I watch Boone in the doorway of my home, looking at Jeremiah as if he could kill the man. But Boone is not a killer. He is a detective. He knows people in ways they don't know themselves.

I glance over at Callahan, who stands with her hands on her holster. MacArthur, the other officer, also stands with his hand on his hip, ready for whatever might happen next.

And the scary truth is I don't know. I never learned how to diffuse Jeremiah's anger. I spent sixteen years married to the man, and yet I never knew how to calm him down. Because once he got angry, he would make sure everyone understood just how mad he was.

But at Garden Temple, he was in charge. He could lay down the law because he had written it. But here in the real world, in Tacoma, Washington, this is not his jurisdiction. And so Boone levels him with his eyes, walking closer, his voice strong and low. Sure.

My heart races as Jeremiah tries to pick Boone apart with his black, beady eyes. Trying to identify who this man is and why he's here.

Boone is a detective. So while he is a man of law, he does not wear a uniform. His badge is not proudly displayed on his chest. And I think how perfectly that fits Boone. He is a man who has control, who has a presence and command, but he doesn't have to wear it on his chest.

"Why are you in my wife's home?" Jeremiah asks Boone.

Boone lifts an eyebrow. "Your wife, huh?" Boone gives him a smug smile. "I'm under the impression that whatever relationship you had with Grace was not legally binding. Do you want to discuss her age at the time of her pregnancy with Abel?"

He could have said so much more. He could have said, *I know what you did to her was illegal, immoral, and wrong on all accounts.* But I understand that Boone does not want to get into the legality of all of that today while Ruthie is missing.

I appreciate Boone's understanding of the situation more than he might ever know. Yes, I want to deal with my past and my children's future with Jeremiah, but not in this moment. Not when so much is at stake, not when Ruthie is gone.

Jeremiah wants to fight. "You can't tell me where I can and cannot go. Grace hasn't asked me to leave."

"Yes, I did," I say, sticking up for myself. Callahan shoots me a glance, her hand still on her hip, her gun at the ready. "I told you to leave, Jeremiah," I say, my voice quaking, "and I meant it."

"You'd want the father of your children out in the cold?" Jeremiah asks. "Come on, Grace. We still have some talking to do."

"No, Jeremiah, we don't," I say, proud of myself in this moment because I am not backing down. I am standing up for myself to the man who has tormented me for so long. I'm grateful that Boone is here, that Callahan is too. I'm grateful for MacArthur.

But right now, I'm mostly grateful for myself.

Earlier today, Boone told me I was a survivor. His words didn't mean as much then as they do right now, because right now I am harnessing the power that they contain. "I want you to go, Jeremiah, and I don't want you to come back."

"Grace, I need to be here when Ruthie comes home, and then I need to take you all back where you belong."

"No," I say. "We don't belong with you. We don't belong *to* you. We are not your property or anyone else's."

Olive's hand is still clasped in mine, and

Abel steps toward his dad. "You heard her. You need to go. Don't touch Bethany."

Jeremiah gives his son a sick, sly smile. "Oh, Abel, have you asked what she wants? It's too late for that. She's already mine."

The word *mine* hangs heavy in the air and I want to yell. I want to scream. I want to wrap my fingers around Jeremiah's neck and squeeze until he cannot breathe. I want to hold him down. I want to grab the gun on Callahan's hip, and I want to shoot a bullet through Jeremiah's head.

I want all sorts of things that are impossible. I want justice. I want to tear down the man who spent so long breaking me. But as I take a long, shallow breath, I know I want something more. I want Ruthie in my arms, safe and protected. And if I do any of the things I'm fantasizing about, I won't have that opportunity.

And her heart belongs to me in ways Jeremiah's never did.

"Go," I say.

Boone pulls open the door. "You heard them. Get the hell out."

Jeremiah shakes his head. "You're going to regret this, Grace."

"No, she won't," Olive says.

"How can you be so sure?" Jeremiah asks his daughter. "How can you be so sure your mother is right and I'm wrong?"

Olive smirks. The veil that was over her eyes for so many years has been lifted. My daughter, she can see.

And that is why we ran a year ago, from him, so she could take in the world for what it truly is.

"I can be sure," she says to her father, "because I stopped believing in you and started believing in myself."

17

After Jeremiah storms out of the house, I run to the window, wanting to watch where he goes. Hating that he is in this neighborhood at all. He is shouting as he walks down my front steps, ranting about bureaucracy and the lost souls who will pay. When he gets in his car and peels out, I exhale with relief. He may say he is angry, but he's not upset enough to stick around and make sure we find Ruthie.

I fall to my knees shaking, sobbing. It's not just that I stood up for myself to a man who's kept me small for most of my life, it's knowing that I don't have an answer about Ruthie.

A hand is on my back. Boone kneels

beside me. "What do you need right now, Gray? What do you need?"

I look at him, tears down my cheeks, shaking my head. "I need Ruthie back," I say. "Where is she, Boone? Who has her? Why do they have her?" My voice is fragile, which matches my heart, shattering with the reality of what we don't know. My eight-year-old daughter is not home, and it's after five o'clock at night. The sun is setting. The clouds are still heavy in the sky, and it would be foolish to think she'll be found in the dead of night. Once everyone goes home to rest, no one will be looking for Ruthie. And where can you look, anyway, once you've gone down every street?

"I know you need Ruthie," Boone tells me. "Everyone who's helping with this case knows you need Ruthie, but are you okay with what just happened? Do you need to talk? Do you—"

I cut him off. "I don't want to talk about Jeremiah. Not now. Later." There's so much to say, but not in this moment. Not when so much is on the line. Abel exhales slowly, and I look up, my eyes landing on my son. "What?" I ask him.

"It's just a lot seeing him here like that.

The way he said Bethany was *his*: it kills me, Mom. It really kills me."

"I know, Abel. I know."

Boone's eyes narrow. "Who's Bethany?" he asks.

Abel, Olive, and I share a glance, not unlike the ones Boone's been sharing with Callahan and York and Truce since this investigation began. A look that says, *We know something we can't tell you. Parts of the investigation that are too grim.*

It sobers me up, reminding me of how most abduction cases go. If the child is not found within twenty-four hours, the odds of her being recovered safely are slim to none. Ruthie could be anywhere right now. She could be across state lines, in another country, on a cargo ship headed south. I don't know. And that's the part that is so painful. The not knowing.

"I'm okay," I say. "I mean, I'm not *okay*, but I'm not crying because of Jeremiah. I'm crying because I stood up to him, because I said what I needed to say, words I waited a year to say—longer, my entire adult life." I stand, smoothing my hands over my hair, reaching for the elastic around my wrist and pulling my hair into a ponytail. "We will talk about Jeremiah later, okay?"

Callahan, Boone, and MacArthur nod. "Of course," Callahan says.

"He may have said he wanted to stay for Ruthie, but I think he realized this was a room of people not in his corner. He's not the kind of person who sticks around where he's not wanted. His entire life is built around being wanted. So"—I press my lips together, shaking my head—"I bet he's already on the freeway headed east."

Olive says she's going to make herself something to eat, and she leaves for the kitchen, Abel following. "So where does that leave us?" I ask.

Just then, Truce enters my home, tipping his head at me.

"Evening, Gray," Truce says, saying hello to the other officers in my presence. "So we got some news," he tells me. "It's good and bad."

"Please, it's not the time to be cryptic," I tell him. "What do you know?"

He lifts up his shoulders, then lets them fall.

"Is it about Cory?" I press.

He shakes his head. "No, Gray. It's about

Jasper. Turns out he has an alibi for last night, and he was horrified to learn about what happened to your little girl."

"How can you be sure?" I ask. "Maybe he sent someone to take Ruthie, and he really has her in his basement or something. They have a really big house. They're really rich and ..."

"We did a thorough search of Jasper's home. He was more than willing to help with the investigation."

Callahan smirks. "So the exact opposite of Cory Jacobson's house and his grandma?"

"Yeah," Truce says. "The exact opposite. Jasper seems like a train wreck, off the record. However, he is not a kidnapper, and he has nothing to do with Ruthie's case."

"How can you be so sure? What was his alibi?" I ask.

Truce shakes his head. "The guy was at an AA meeting. His sponsor verified and seems like it all checks out."

"I didn't even know Jasper had a drinking problem," I say.

"Sounds like he did a stint in rehab a long time ago. He's been sober for a decade. Was scared of spiraling after his wife died. Went back for support. So it all tracks," Truce finishes explaining.

"How did he sound?" I ask. "Upset? Why was he outside my house? What was he here for, circling around my neighborhood for two days watching us, watching me?"

"It's a pity, really. I mean, losing someone is hard." He glances over at Boone at that. "I think we all can understand that. And he was just trying to process. You were the last person who saw his wife alive, and so maybe he felt comfort in the idea of you, of seeing you, your girls. He says he was scared something bad would happen to you. After all, he'd just found out everything with his wife's murder, so he wasn't sure if you were in any danger and wasn't certain that the police could protect you."

"He was looking out for us?" I ask, feeling like that matches Jasper more than the idea of him being a child abductor. I remember him sitting in that chair at the wELLEness Center so vividly, his shoulders slumped, his face in his palms, sobbing. The unexpected loss of his wife breaking him. How was that only days ago?

My eyes feel heavy at the weight of the last few weeks, wondering if there's ever going to be a time my load will be lighter. I don't want it to be if Ruthie's not here. "So you're saying we've lost a suspect," I say.

Truce nods. "That's exactly what I'm saying. Jasper did not take your daughter."

"So, Cory," I say, landing on the teenage neighbor's name, "he's the one who has her."

"Well," Boone says, "I guess we'll know the truth of that soon enough."

18

Jeremiah's visit brought up a lot of my worst fears, but seeing Olive and Abel at the kitchen table, eating dinner together, lessens them a bit. They are looking at a photo album I printed for the girls this past Christmas.

It's a collection of photographs from the past year of the three of us beginning our life in Tacoma. The three of us down at Ruston Way, riding bikes in the summer. A spontaneous trip to Lake Crescent, up in the Olympic Mountains before school started. We'd rented a kayak and paddled around the lake, not having any idea what we were doing, but laughing the entire time.

There are pictures that I made them take

before they started a new school year, new backpacks on, new clothing. They said they didn't need all that fuss, but that was coming from children who grew up never having photos taken of themselves. Never dressing up for a special occasion, wearing hand-me-downs and eating leftovers, going to a one-room schoolhouse where one of the sister wives taught them to read so they could read the Bible.

I notice Abel's expressions as he looks through the pictures, running his fingertips over the images, asking his sister questions. She laughs explaining these documented days in detail. What it's been like living with *just Mom*, as she puts it.

Callahan and I stand side by side, looking out the big window in the living room. Streetlamps shine light on the road; the snow is mostly gone, and now there is no reason that the search party should be delayed besides, of course, the fact it's getting dark.

"Your kids," Callahan starts, "they're pretty sweet."

"Yeah, they are," I say. "Olive is so good to me. She's my voice of reason, you know? And without her, I would have never been able to figure out what was going on with the supplements that Elle was selling."

Callahan nods. "I heard about that case. Pretty interesting. How did Olive help?"

I smile. "She's in science club at school and they had a whole experiment where they were testing out supplements, trying to figure out what was organic or not. She discovered that the wELLEness products were full of placebos and that the company wasn't selling much more than a fancy bottle."

"And you're saying she grew up in a place where there wasn't a lot of formal education?" Callahan asks tentatively. I know she's tiptoeing around her real question, wanting to know exactly where we lived, how we lived, and why.

"Olive was always smart. You know how some kids just pick things up easily? And I'm not saying this to be rude about any other children, but she was the kind of kid who, at three, was teaching herself to read. At five, she was bored with addition. She was always thinking, curious. She would collect bugs in Mason jars to study them, drawing their pictures with her colored pencils. I knew she needed more than what she was being offered. Our life with Jeremiah was very small. And Olive, I mean, look at her." I turn to face the kitchen table. "She's magnificent."

Callahan nods. "She's lucky to have you, someone who sees all that talent."

"Yeah," I say slowly. "And now I'm just wondering, am I ever going to be able to help Ruthie discover her talents? Foster them? It's been twenty-four hours, Callahan. Do you think my little girl is ever coming back?"

"I don't know," Callahan says. "Our hope right now is that Cory's interview is going well. And by well, I mean informatively."

I nod, understanding what she means. It's not that I wish Cory ill, but I do hope whatever he says to the officers at the police station sheds some light on this case.

Just then, York comes back inside my house. "Hey, Gray. I wanted you to know that your neighbors, Granger and Bart, are about to head up a search party. If you want to go out with them, now would be a good time."

"Really?" I ask. "You'll let me go?"

He smiles. "Hey, I'm not as big of a hardass as you seem to think I am. I'm a good guy, you know? Better than Boone, really."

Callahan laughs. "Right. Didn't I see your car parked outside that strip club on Sixth last week?"

He chuckles. "That was not my car."

"Oh, really?" Callahan says. "Because I could swear your Bronco has a bumper sticker that says *Save a horse, ride a cowboy*."

"Whatever," York says, shaking his head. Not saying yes or no. And that pretty much answers everything.

Not wanting to wait for him to change his mind, I put on my winter coat, my gloves, zip up my jacket. "Hey kids," I say. They turn to face me. They've warmed up the lasagna someone dropped off, along with garlic bread and salad. They've just started to dig in. "I'm going to head out for an hour to help with the search. You guys stay here in case there is an update, okay? And call me if there's any news." Turning to Callahan, I ask, "You'll stay here with them, won't you?"

"Of course," she says. "I'll be right here. Go, get some fresh air. See your friends. They'll help bolster your determination, and that's what you need right now, Gray."

I want to hug her. I know she's a police officer and we just met, but I still want to give Charlie Callahan a big old squeeze and tell her thank you.

Instead, she smiles and I smile back, and I

suppose a smile is worth as much as a hug sometimes.

"Okay," I say, suddenly with a stomach full of nerves, scared of the unknown, of finding something other than my daughter alive.

York tells me to stick with him. I take in the neighborhood as we walk, noticing officers holding leashes of the dogs that are now out on the search. York explains how they've been trained to help pick up Ruthie's scent. As we walk down the road, in front of the mobile patrol unit at the gas station parking lot, I see a group of my neighbors, Granger among them. "Hey, Gray," he says. "You're able to come out?"

I nod. "Yeah, thankfully. I've been wanting to come help all day, but ..."

"No, no. Don't explain. I understand, you have a lot going on, and damn, I'm just so sorry."

I blink back tears, feeling the support of my community in a way I never expected. Sure, I lived in a small compound for most of my life, and I had sister wives who knew me intimately, and a community at Garden Temple that was close-knit, but it's different here because there is no looming shadow of fear.

Here, intentions are pure. So, when Granger gives me a quick hug, I hug him back, thanking him for leading the search. Bart, Luna's husband, hands me a flashlight. "It's getting dark," he says, "but that means we can pick up things that we wouldn't have seen during the day. Things that Ruthie would have come across last night."

This is just about the time she was taken ... I look at my watch. It's 6:00 p.m., when Ruthie took out the trash. If I would've come straight from work to the house and not stopped to get fake identification for Abel, I would have been here and Ruthie wouldn't be gone. And everything would be different.

I swallow away that guilt, knowing it won't serve me in this moment. There's a group of eight people gathered, and Granger explains the route we're going to take. Just as we're beginning to start our trek, I hear Callahan coming through York's radio.

I stop, turning to him. "What is it?" I ask, hoping it has something to do with Ruthie.

He shakes his head. "I'm sorry, Gray. I thought it was a good idea for you to come out, but ..."

"But what?" My voice flares, and the rest of the group turns, realizing that I'm upset.

"It's your daughter, Olive. She needs you home."

"What's happened?"

"She's upset because her brother—your son—he's telling her he's leaving, going home. She needs you to stop him."

19

"I'M SO SORRY," I tell the volunteers that I just began walking with. "I need to get back to my house."

"Don't worry about it, Gray," Granger says, his voice filled with compassion.

"Okay. I'm so sorry. I've just got to go help my daughter. She's really upset."

A woman shakes her head. "Don't apologize. Go do what you need to do, and we will stay here doing what we can do. We're going to help you," she says. "Hold on to hope, Gray."

I walk away realizing that was Olive's friend Tomas's mother, the dean of their school. We met earlier today, but it feels like a lifetime ago.

My heart is flooded with gratitude as York and I jog back to the house. The idea that so many people have spent their entire day helping us is so overwhelming.

"I know everyone's committed to this search and that gives me ease," I tell York. "But I really did want to go out with them. Do my part and help."

"Callahan said your daughter sounded pretty upset."

"Yeah, which is unlike Olive. She's the levelheaded one in our family."

"Where is home for your son?" he asks.

I run a hand over the base of my neck. Walking more quickly. "Home is in Eastern Washington with his father."

"Oh right. I heard about that earlier."

"Word travels fast in your department," I say.

"Yeah, well, under the circumstances."

I nod, understanding. Under the circumstances, there are no secrets. Under these circumstances, every overheard word uttered in my household is documented. Callahan has had her tablet in hand since the moment we met. Making notes, adding them to the growing file on my dysfunctional family.

When I get inside, Olive is using both hands to hold her brother back. "You can't leave!" she shouts. "We need you."

Callahan stands with her eyes wide, listening, not jumping in. And I understand if it's a sibling dispute, she probably doesn't think it's her place to interject.

Of course, it would have been different on the compound. A sister wife has just as much authority over the children in the household as their biological mother, but this is not a sister-wife situation. This is as far from it as you can get, actually.

"What's going on?" I ask. "When I left, you were having a sweet moment eating your dinner and looking at family photos."

"We were," Olive says, "until Abel decided to take a phone call from Bethany and start act like a freaking lunatic. He's leaving, Mom. He says he's going. Like now."

"You're not going anywhere," I say. "Abel, it's almost seven at night. It's pitch dark. You don't have a car. You don't have a driver's license, and you're sure as heck not catching a bus to Moses Lake. You're saying here until your sister is found, and then we will deal with Bethany."

Abel shakes his head, angry. "You don't understand, Mom. I have to go. I have to go *now*. Give me your keys."

"I'm not giving you my keys," I say, shocked at his determination. "Why is this so urgent? More urgent than your sister?"

"It's not that I don't want to stay here to help look for Ruthie, but we can't even look. I'm not allowed out of this house."

"No," I say, "you can. You can go meet Granger and Bart right now," I decide, wanting to dangle a carrot to keep him here. "They're all doing a search tonight, and they're only two blocks away. Go with them now, Abel. If you want to help, you can help."

"Can I?" Olive asks.

"No," I say, "you can't. You're saying here."

"Why? Because I'm a girl?"

"Yes," I say, "because you're a girl."

"Abel's only fifteen."

He glares at her. "I'll be sixteen in two weeks."

"That doesn't make you a man," Olive smarts back. "This isn't Garden Temple. You're still a minor in the real world."

"Well, I'm not going to stay in the real world. I'm going to Moses Lake, and I'm getting Bethany."

"And then what?" I say. "You think you're going to live happily ever after with her and your father? That's going to go real well. Won't it, Abel?" My voice is firm and tight, hard even. Callahan and York are stunned into silence. I can't say more about the Bethany and Jeremiah situation because that would complicate matters that cannot afford to be complicated until Ruthie is found.

Matters that involve the father of my children planning to bind himself to another woman in a few days. The woman my son is in love with. God, my whole life sounds like a soap opera. Or a horror story.

"Abel. Let's start at the beginning. You got a call. What happened next? How did Bethany contact you, when earlier today Bethany wasn't taking calls?"

"I don't know why she called me. But she did," he says, reaching for the phone in his pocket and shoving it toward me.

"She did?"

"Yeah, she was able to steal the phone back from Lydia and ... Mom, are you even listening?"

"Yes, I'm listening," I say, glancing at Olive, who has tears in her eyes. She's shaking her head, on the verge of falling apart. I reach out and pull her into my arms. "Olive," I say. "I'm right here. We're right here. We're okay."

"But everyone's shouting. You know I hate it when you shout."

"How often do I shout?" I ask.

"You used to. You used to be mad all the time back at the compound. You and Naomi would always fight. And you and Lydia, and I hated it. I didn't want to leave when you made us go. But then I realized when you're here, you don't scream because you're not mad all the time. You're not scared all the time. And ..." She starts shaking, stepping away from me. Not wanting the embrace I'm offering. "And I don't like it. I don't like it when you yell. I don't like it when you fight with Abel. I want everything to go back to what it was a week ago." Olive shakes her head, angry. "No, two weeks ago. Or actually, I want it to go back to a month ago before everything happened with Patrick, and before everything happened with Ruthie, when we were just the three of us, happy."

"See," Abel says. "She wants me to go. She wants it to just be you guys. So I'll go. I'll go get Bethany and leave you guys alone."

"No," I say, "that's not what I want. It's not what Olive wants either."

"I want you to stay, Abel," Olive cries. "I just don't want you to fight with Mom anymore. It's already so scary. I just want ... I just want Ruthie home, and I want you to stay and help us find her. I don't want you to leave, Abel. Not when we've already lost so much. Don't you want to be in the family pictures? Don't you want to be a part of our family memories?" Olive pleads with her brother. I've never seen her like this. So torn up. So utterly spent. But how could I have? We have never been in a situation like this before.

"It's not that simple," Abel tells us.

"Why isn't it?" I ask. "Why isn't it as simple as you telling Bethany we'll come help her once Ruthie is found?"

"Because," Abel says, swallowing, the tears filling his eyes now too. "Because, Mom, Bethany is pregnant."

"Pregnant?" The room goes quiet. There's nothing to hear but the shock reverberating off the walls. "Did you know this?" I ask Olive.

She shakes her head. "No, he just took the phone call in the bathroom, and then when he came out, he said he was leaving." She turns to her brother. "She's pregnant?"

"Yeah," Abel says. "And she's scared."

I swallow, remembering when I found out I was pregnant. I hadn't understood that I needed a pregnancy test. I just understood that my bleeding had stopped. I understood that my breasts were tender and my belly was growing round, and after a few months I started piecing it together. I was more than four months pregnant before I told Jeremiah, before I opened my mouth and said, "I think I'm with child."

The look of joy on his face was the purest pleasure I've ever seen from him. He had gone to the drugstore and gotten pregnancy tests, making me take them. After we confirmed I was really carrying his child, he announced it at service. Telling all the congregation at Garden Temple about the miracle.

But was it a miracle? I was a fertile girl with a husband who was lying with me each night.

That's not a miracle.

Now I have more words for it. Rape. Nonconsensual intercourse. Molestation. My innocence taken from a pedophile.

But I didn't have those words then. With horror it dawns on me—does Bethany have those words too?

“Abel?” I ask, “The baby, is it yours? Or is it his?”

20

ABEL'S EYES go dark and my heart stops. Willing, praying. Needing him to say his own name and not the name of his father. He blinks a few times, rubs his eyes. I see the heartache etched in them, and I feel his pain even though I don't completely understand it. Finally, he opens his mouth.

"She's only ever been with me," he admits.

Olive gasps, stunned by the confession. Her indoctrination at Garden Temple preached a solid and clear message about purity, and it did not include sex before marriage. Which is what Abel has just confessed to.

At first, I expect Olive to shake her head in disappointment because when we first left Garden Temple, she had a hard time. This whole year has been hard. It's only recently that she's turned a corner and has been able to see the cracks in her history.

Thankfully, she doesn't say anything hurtful. When she speaks, compassion is written in her voice, and I know it's the story of her heart.

“Oh, Abel,” she says, “you really want to get back to Bethany, don't you?”

He nods. “I understand why this is complicated, but ...”

“Abel,” I say, adamant. “You cannot go to her tonight. I can't drive you. You're not getting on a bus so late. For many reasons you can’t go. For one, it would raise some red flags we don't need raised right now.”

“What do you mean, red flags?” Abel asks.

“We have to play this cool, Abel. Jeremiah was here, and so his wedding to her isn’t going to happen tonight. We can’t go barging into Garden Temple and run off with Bethany. We need a plan.”

“I don’t want to wait,” he says, running his

hands through his hair. "I want her with me. Safe."

"I know you do, sweetie. But we cannot help Bethany when we are trying to fight for Ruthie. Do you understand? I know you want to go to her. I know you care for her and want to help, but Abel, you can't do it in the middle of the night. If you left now, it would be midnight when you showed up at the compound, and what do you think would happen? You think her father would let her go?"

"He doesn't know that she's pregnant. Nobody does. Only I do. Only we do," he says. "Mom, I have to ..."

"I know you have to help her as soon as you can, but right now you cannot. You're staying here, Abel, in Tacoma, and we're finding your sister. Do you understand?"

All three of us are crying now, and honestly, I think Callahan is too.

The front door opens, and Boone steps inside, assessing the situation. I wipe my face, batting at the tears. "Why do you always show up when I'm at my worst?" I ask.

"You want me to go?"

I shake my head. "No," I say, "I want you

to tell me something good because right now everything feels like it's falling apart. Please, Boone, tell me something good."

He looks over at Abel, who's clearly been crying. "You okay?"

Abel runs a hand over his face. "Just need to find my sister so I can go help my girlfriend. She's in trouble."

"Trouble, like nine-one-one?" Boone asks him, leveling. "Trouble like she needs to go to the emergency room?"

Abel shakes his head no. "Not that kind of trouble."

"Okay. Then she'll be okay for now," Boone says, diffusing the situation. "So you're going to stay put," he tells Abel. "So are you, Olive, and we're going to stay in this house, and we're going to find Ruthie, okay? That's what we're going to do. Callahan's here, Truce, York, you know the crew. We're all here for you. We're here. Gray, we're here," he says, his eyes finding mine. "Gray, you with me?"

I nod, trembling, falling apart internally but trying to remain strong. I squeeze my fists tight. I'm alive, I'm alive. I'm here.

"Okay," Boone says. "So you said you needed something?" he asks me. "You needed something to happen with Ruthie? Because we got it."

"What do you have?" I ask, defeated in every possible way. My hands fly up into the air. "What do you have, Boone, that's going to help? Do you have Ruthie? Is she here? Is she in your car? Is she coming home?" I ask, wiping my nose.

"No," he says, "but we have a lead and it's promising."

"Oh yeah? Just like Jasper was promising?" I spit at him. "Just like Jeremiah was promising?"

"Hey," Boone says, "I'm not the bad guy here. I'm helping. I came with news I knew you needed."

"News? What news?" I ask, my whole body on high alert.

"We found Cory's hideout."

My heart pounds. "Was Ruthie there?"

He shakes his head. "I'm sorry, Gray."

"What did you find there?" I ask.

"We found a few items of note, mainly Ruthie's winter coat."

I gasp, hating the thought of my little girl in the cold without her coat to keep her warm.

"Callahan, how you doing?" Boone asks,

giving me a moment to get out my frustration.

"I'm doing fine." She twists her lips, unconvincing. "Actually, I'm going to make some coffee."

I glare at her. "Did you already know about Ruthie's coat?"

Callahan nods. "Yeah, actually I did, Gray. It's my job to know."

"And you didn't tell me?" I ask. "You're just keeping secrets from me?"

"Gray, I'm not the enemy either. Boone and I are here to help you, but we don't have to stay. We're here if you want us, okay? Do you want me here?" she asks. "Because I can keep an eye on you from a patrol car in the driveway if you don't want me in the house. I really don't want to be where I'm not wanted." Her words are so calm, so collected, and so ridiculously chill, I want to smack her.

But more than that, I want to hug her.

How do I care so much about a woman I've just met? Wanting to hug her twice within a few hours seems absurd. I'm not a touchy-feely person. But I feel this way because she is the voice of reason I need. I'm too caught up in Boone. She knows it and I know it. He knows it too. I care for Boone in ways that terrify me. Callahan, on the other hand, is the friend I've never had.

"So," she says, "I'm going to make the coffee, and I'm going to let Boone fill you in, and then you're going to come in here, and you're going to get one of those chocolate chip cookies someone left because they're really damn good. And you're going to eat it, and you're going to drink some coffee, and then you are going to talk this through with me, okay? Olive, Abel, you're going to join your mom in a few minutes with me in the kitchen, okay? I'll pour you some milk, and we're going to get ourselves together, okay? That's the plan. That's what we're going to do right now."

I nod, wiping my eyes. "Okay. Thank you," I say, embarrassed for my outburst, for my breakdown.

She waves it off, goes in the kitchen. She's not looking for an apology. Her job is to keep me in one piece and God, that woman's doing it well.

"Gray, Olive, Abel—Cory has a bunker," Boone says. "That's what we're calling it. It's really a shipping container down by the train tracks. He has a little setup there, a glorified hangout with a few old armchairs, a mattress. Hell, he has those LED strip lights hanging around that all these Gen Z-ers are into."

Olive smirks.

"So he has this fort, if you will," Boone explains. "And inside this fort of his, we found a few things. A few things that are alarming and raise a lot of questions, okay?"

"Okay," I say, my stomach turning at his calm demeanor. No one is this serious if it's good news.

"The coat described by your family during the intake yesterday when we were creating the file. And another one of her hair clips. Those items were on the floor beside the bed and ..."

"Oh my God," I say. "Cory took her there? Then where did he take her?"

Boone coughs. "I'm headed over to the police station right now to do an interview that's going to be a lot more like an interrogation if I'm being completely honest with you. And I am, Gray; I'm being honest with you. I don't know where this interview is going to go, but I can promise you I'll let you know as soon as I have an answer, okay?"

I nod. "Okay." I bite down hard on my

bottom lip, and Olive squeezes my hand tight. Abel rakes his hands through his hair.

"God, I'm such a goddamn idiot," he says, his language shocking me, Olive too. Even Boone looks surprised. "I'm sorry, Mom. God, I'm such a shitty son. I told you I was going to go and then this. I couldn't have left you like this. I'm sorry, Mom. I'm staying put. I'll tell Bethany I'll come as soon as I can, but not until we have Ruthie, okay?"

"Okay," I say, relieved and terrified and heartbroken all at once.

And my boy, who truly is nearly a man, a father even, wraps me in a hug and holds me up, and it probably should be the reverse, the mother comforting the child, but right now it's Abel comforting me. Olive is holding us both, and the tears keep falling. There's fear so deep inside of me, I'm scared it's going to swallow me whole.

Eventually we step back, and Boone, who's wiping his eyes with the flat of his palm, looks at me. "I made you a promise and I plan on keeping it."

"Thank you," I say, my voice cracking, shattering. But I don't say anymore. The things Boone and I need to say are not even things that I have words for. Not yet. Maybe not ever. Maybe the interview will determine that. Our fate.

I don't know much, but I am certain of one thing: if anyone is going to question the person who kidnapped my daughter, I want it to be Orion Boone.

21

Boone tells the kids and me to go grab those cookies Callahan mentioned.

"They sound pretty good," he adds, and we file into the kitchen. Callahan is reaching for a few mugs in one of the kitchen cupboards, and asks Boone if he'd like some too.

"Actually," Boone says, "do you have any travel mugs, Gray?"

"Uh, yeah," I tell him, "I do." I walk toward Callahan and open the cupboard next to her, reaching for one.

"Do you have two travel mugs, by any chance?" he asks.

"I do. Who are they for?" I turn to him and he shrugs.

"Cory Jacobson had a pre-interview at the station, prepping us for when I go in for the interrogation. To be honest, I think having you there might be helpful."

"Me?" I ask, surprised. "Really?"

"Well, we have a fancy two-way mirror, so you can stay on one side and watch."

"Watch as you interrogate him?" I ask.

Callahan tsks. "You think that's a good idea?"

"Obviously," Boone says, "otherwise I wouldn't be asking her."

"All right," she says, nodding. "I can see how that could be helpful. Maybe this kid's account will trigger something."

"Exactly," Boone says. "So let's get a cookie and coffee to go, all right?"

I look over at Olive and Abel. "Will you guys be okay here?" I ask. "I know earlier when I left, it got pretty tense."

Abel shakes his head. "Mom, that won't happen again. I'm really sorry, for everything."

I reach out and give him a quick hug. "I know you are, honey. I'm sorry too."

"You don't need to apologize for anything," Olive says stoically. "For anything.

I mean, everything that's going on *is* pretty insane."

I smile, kissing her forehead. "You're right, it is pretty insane, and hopefully it'll end soon."

I grab a cookie and break it in two, taking a bite. "These are good."

"Kendall dropped them off," Olive says. "Isn't it crazy how nice everyone in this neighborhood is?"

"Yeah," I say, "we're really lucky."

Callahan smiles at that. "Okay, take your coffee, and go before you get too sentimental for your own good."

"You'll stay here with the kids?" I ask.

She nods. "There's nowhere else I'd rather be."

This time I don't hold back. Twice tonight I've wanted to hug this woman and this time I do. I pull her in for a hug, catching her off guard.

"What was that for?" she asks when I step back.

I pour coffee creamer into my to-go cup, adding a splash to Boone's knowing that's how he takes his. "It's for being the most normal woman I've ever gotten to know."

She laughs. "That's not usually the way people describe me."

"No?" I ask, looking over at Boone. "How do people usually describe Charlie Callahan?"

He laughs despite the intense day we've had, and his laugh fills my heart with hope. The kind of hope I need right now.

"Most people would say lucky Callahan is a bit of a hard-ass."

I smile. "I've always gotten along with hard-asses."

"That so?" Boone asks. "Sounds promising."

I bite back my smile, knowing his words are more loaded than either of us are ready to admit. With our coffee cups in hand and our cookies perched on top of the lids, we head out into the cold night. In his car, I buckle up, smiling when the radio turns on and begins blasting classical music.

"You're pretty old school," I say.

He chuckles. "Yeah, I am. Music with lyrics stresses me out. And when I'm driving, I like to clear my head."

"I can relate," I say, "that's why I like working at the library shelving books, just me and my cart going down the rows in quiet.

Rarely does anyone ever talk to me, and it's not that I'm antisocial, but I like being able to breathe and think in peace."

Boone drives down my neighborhood, and we pass the mobile command unit. I can't help but stare at the groups of people still crowded around. There's a news van parked at the gas station. A reporter is giving an interview, asking questions of my neighbor Luna.

"Does that bother you?" Boone asks.

"No, it doesn't. She's really a nice person, and I need nice people in my life, in my corner."

"Don't we all," Boone says.

We drive in silence to the police station, and when we get there, I ask if there's anything I should know before going in.

"More than anything," Boone says, "just stay calm. Stay patient with the process. When I ask questions, the intention or my motivation might not always be clear, but just trust me and my job, okay? I know it's going to kill you to not be able to say anything until it's over."

"And there's really no way he'll know I'm watching?"

"None," Boone says. "He might make a guess, but no. It's completely private."

Inside the station, I keep my eyes down, not interested in the pitying looks of the officers. Still, after my past habit of avoiding the law at all costs, it is strange to be here so openly, so plainly.

They know who I am, where I live, what I do for a living. They know my daughter is gone. They know I've lied before. Maybe they think I'm lying again. But none of that really matters because I'm not a suspect in my daughter's kidnapping. Cory Jacobson, on the other hand, is.

I'm left in a small room with a few chairs, and there's another officer with me. We exchange hellos but nothing else. Boone tells me to let the officer know if anything in Cory's interview sparks something and that he'd like to know if that happens before continuing.

"All right," I say, "I understand."

Alone in the room, I watch as Cory Jacobson, the neighbor down the street, is brought in for questioning.

"Why isn't he cuffed?" I ask the officer beside me.

"He hasn't been charged with anything yet."

Cory sits in a chair, and it's several minutes before Boone joins him.

When he does, I notice Boone has that to-go mug from my kitchen in one hand and half a chocolate chip cookie in the other. He's finishing it as he sits down.

I take Boone in, in a way I never have before. I can stare objectively without feeling weird. In the past I compared him to a mountain man, which appealed to me. But now I see it's more than simply his broad shoulders and beard. It's something feral, something unmoored that draws me to him. His past heartbreak, certainly, but I know there's so much more to Boone than what happened to him when he lost his daughter and ended things with his wife. There's a whole life I don't know about. That I want to know about.

I just pray that there will be space for happiness in my life eventually. Because right now, there is little to be happy about. My focus turns to Cory. He's fidgeting, tapping his foot. His eyes are darting left to right.

"This is really stupid, you know," he groans before Boone says a word. Boone simply takes a drink of his coffee and sets it down.

"Stupid, yeah?" Boone asks.

Cory grunts. "Yeah, it's really fucking stupid. I didn't do anything, and there's no reason for me to be here."

"No reason?" Boone runs a hand over his jaw. "That's interesting. So why *do* you think you're here?"

Cory sits up straighter. "You want to talk to me about what happened to that little girl, Ruthie."

"We've interviewed a lot of people about this, about her," Boone says. "The pieces are coming together really quickly, and if you had anything to do with this, you should tell me now."

Cory scoffs. "I have nothing to say to you about Ruthie. I don't even know her last name."

"It's West," Boone says, "Ruthie West."

"Yeah, well, I feel bad for the kid, but I don't know what happened to her."

"You sure? I want to ask you a few questions regarding your knowledge about the event. Do you know when it happened? When Ruthie was abducted?"

"Yeah, last night. I saw the news, but I

don't know where she was taken or like, what time or anything."

"Well, why do you think someone would do this?" Boone asks.

Cory groans, dropping his head back, shifting in his seat. He's thin, with dark circles under his brown eyes, his long, stringy hair past his shoulders, and he keeps flicking his fingers with his thumb. Antsy. I know Boone is watching all of this, taking it in. What does it say? Do Cory's gestures mean he's guilty or innocent? I don't know enough about interrogation to answer the question.

"I don't know why someone would do this. Probably because they're a sick fuck? I don't know, maybe it was her dad or something, or like, some creep at school."

"You think creeps at school would do this?"

"I don't know. I don't know why anyone would do this. Maybe someone hated her. Maybe the kidnapper was some insane dude. I don't know." He leans forward in his chair, keeping eye contact with Boone. "All I know is I never thought about doing something this bad."

"So what do you think should happen to the person who did do this to Ruthie West?"

"Uh, I don't know. It's not up to me."

"Who is it up to?"

"I don't know, like the courts or something? Why don't you do your job and just find her? Because she can tell you I didn't do this."

"You didn't answer the question," Boone persists. "What should happen to the person who did this to Ruthie?"

Cory shrugs. "You should like ... give him the death penalty? I mean, it's pretty fucked up to hurt a kid."

"Hurt?" Boone asks, voice raised. "Did you ever think of hurting Ruthie, even if you didn't go through with it?"

"No. I mean, no I didn't."

"Would you be willing to take a polygraph test to verify that you just told me the truth?"

"Sure. I don't care. Do whatever you want."

"How do you think you would do on a polygraph regarding the abduction of Ruthie?"

He shakes his head, running his fingers through his hair. "I don't know. I'm really nervous. I hate cops."

"Why do you hate cops?" Boone asks.

"You know my priors. It's all fucked up. You're always looking to cause trouble where there isn't any."

"You've shoplifted. You attempted to used a fake ID to buy liquor. That doesn't sound like nothing." Cory doesn't speak, just shrugs. "If we can identify the person who did this to Ruthie, do you think they should be given a second chance?"

"No," Cory says quickly. "Of course not."

"So, you know that we found your shipping container, correct?"

Cory snorts. "Not too hard to find considering it's a block behind my house, by the railroad tracks on Prescott Avenue, and there's a giant spray-painted X on the door."

"And do you know what we found inside?" Boone asks.

Cory twists his lips, biting down. "I heard you found the kid's coat or something."

"Yeah. We found her coat and one of her hair clips, and it was on your mattress, in fact."

"So?" Cory says. "I didn't take her there."

"Okay, so where were you last night at six o'clock?"

"I was just hanging out by myself."

"Where? Because your grandma says you weren't home."

"I know. I was at my hangout."

"The shipping container?" Boone asks to clarify.

"Yeah. I like to go there sometimes just to chill. My grandma can be whack, and I don't like to be there when she's watching TV. So I go to my place. Sleep there sometimes too."

"So you were alone at your shipping container at the time Ruthie was taken. And later, we found her personal effects in this same shipping container where you were alone."

"Someone planted them," Cory says. "I have no idea how they got there. All I'm saying is it wasn't me. It wasn't me."

"All right," Boone says. "That's enough for now." He leaves Cory alone in the interrogation room and walks into the room where I'm sitting at the edge of my seat, listening closely to everything.

"What do you think?" I ask Boone.

"I don't know," Boone says. "The kid has nothing for us to go on. His shipping container wasn't locked; anyone could have gotten in there. There is no camera footage showing anything."

"Maybe she's in his basement or something. Did someone go through his house?"

"Yes," Boone says. "There's nothing inside his house."

"But there were her things in the container, and there were her things in his backyard. I mean, obviously ..."

"Obviously nothing," Boone says. "Gray, maybe it was a bad idea having you come down here."

"Bad idea? No, it was a good idea. Go back in there and ask him where Ruthie is. Please."

Boone places his hands on both my arms. "Gray, I'll go ask him that if that's what you need me to do. I'm telling you, though, at this moment I have nothing to go on. His alibi was that he was alone."

"What kind of alibi is that?"

Boone shakes his head, leaving me alone in the room with the other officer. I sit back down, watching as Boone reenters, sitting opposite Cory.

"I'm going to ask you something pretty straight," he says. "Do you know where Ruthie is?"

"No," Cory says adamantly. "I have no fucking clue where Ruthie is. I don't even think I would know Ruthie if I passed her on the street. She's a kid in the neighborhood. Cool. I don't exactly hang out with six-year-olds."

"Eight," Boone says. "Ruthie is eight."

"I didn't take her," Cory says, his voice punctuated with fear.

"We're finished here," Boone says, calling in an officer to take Cory back to holding.

My shoulders fall, frustrated. I wanted an answer, and instead, I am simply spinning in a circle.

22

BOONE DRIVES ME HOME, and with his car parked in my driveway, I ask him what happens next.

"There's more here with Cory," he tells me. "I'm going to question his grandma again. Find out who his friends are, any other places he might've been hanging out."

"Do you think it was a waste of time?" I ask. "That interrogation."

"No, nothing's a waste of time," Boone says. "And there's something he isn't saying. I intend to find out what that is."

I swallow. "It's weird that her things were in his hideout, don't you think?"

Boone nods. "Yeah. It doesn't add up, does it?"

I shake my head. "No. But not much adds up anymore, does it?" I drop my head into my hands. "I'm so tired, Boone. I'm so tired."

"I know," he says. He takes my hand and holds it. I swallow, and suddenly the car feels too small, too tight, too quiet. "You're going to be okay, Gray."

"Am I?" I ask Boone again, for the dozenth time today. "Am I going to be okay? Living life without Ruthie is impossible to imagine."

"I know," Boone says. "We're going to find her, and you're going to be able to have a happy life. From everything I've gathered about you, you've been waiting a long-ass time for that."

"A happy life," I say. "Really, you think that's even possible?"

"I believe anything is possible," Boone says.

I squeeze his hand. "I hope you're right." I get out of the car and enter the house, knowing it's nearing midnight. The house is silent. I see Olive curled up in an armchair, her head resting on a pillow. A throw blanket draped over her body. I lean down, kissing her head, smoothing her hair. She stirs ever so slightly, but stays sleeping. Abel is sprawled out on the couch, his body so long and so lean, it's insane to imagine him coming from me. He's snoring softly, just like his father.

An officer is in the kitchen. "I'm MacArthur," he says. "We met earlier."

"Where's Charlie?" I ask.

"She went home for a few hours to shower and get some rest. She'll be back, though, by morning."

"That's good," I say. "She should get some sleep."

"What about you?" he asks. "Do you need some rest?" He nods over to the coffeepot. "Or do you need another cup of coffee?"

I shake my head. "I don't need anything. I'm just going to head upstairs and check some phone messages."

"All right," he says. "I'll be in the living room."

I nod, grateful that there's a police officer here keeping watch. Upstairs, I wash my face, my hands gripping the counter as I look at myself in the mirror, trying to figure out what I'm supposed to do. It's the dead of night, and the search is paused, which I completely understand. Everyone is running on fumes after thirty hours of nonstop searching.

I'm in no place to sleep, no place to rest. I'm all cried out too. I don't have the desire to reply to the texts from my neighbors wishing me more positive thoughts and good vibes. It's not that they're not worth anything, but at this point, it's not enough. I need more. I need to do something.

My attempt at going out on a search party this evening was cut short, and I know tomorrow, once the neighborhood is full of police officers and news cameras and well-intentioned friends, I won't have any time to myself, any time to look for Ruthie on my own.

The flashlight Bart gave me earlier is still in my jacket and it gives me an idea. I walk down the stairs quietly. "I'm just going to get some fresh air," I tell MacArthur, who's in the living room.

He nods. "Don't go far," he says.

"I won't," I say. "I just need to breathe."

"I'll stay here; don't worry about them," he says, nodding to the kids.

"Thank you," I say softly. When I left Garden Temple with the girls, I didn't have permission. I left because I knew it was what was necessary.

It's necessary now too. I slip out the front door. It's not fresh air I'm after; I am a mother on a mission.

23

I TURN RIGHT, cutting past the Jacobsons' house on the corner, crossing the railroad tracks on Prescott. There's a long line of shipping containers, and I'm not sure which one is Cory's, but it doesn't take long to narrow it down. Only one is marked with an X, which is a little too obvious. Then again, Cory doesn't seem like the brightest bulb in the bunch.

As I step closer to the muted orange shipping container marked with the X, I notice it is circled with yellow crime scene tape. I look around, surprised there isn't a cop out here. They are probably all a few streets over, at the mobile unit. Considering it's one in the morning, it makes sense. The entire city appears to be asleep. My children are; my neighbors are; Cory may be too, alone in a holding cell waiting to be questioned again. The longer we go without answers about what happened to Ruthie, there will be more heat on him to confess to the crime that might change my life.

The soles of my shoes crunch against the gravel, and I press my hands to the door marked X, hoping it budges and I can pull it open. It does. Clicking on the flashlight, I quickly drag it across the interior of the large metal container. It's empty of people, and I let out a long, slow breath at that.

I hear a voice though, close, and I turn, flashlight on. I see two young men walking closer, in baggy jeans with knit caps on their heads.

Holding the flashlight steady on them, they lift their hands up, laughing, a bottle of liquor in one of their hands.

"Oh shit," they say. "Uh, we got to run." And they do: they run off into the night.

I mutter something under my breath that would probably horrify my children, should horrify me. Assuming those boys were just drunk teenagers, I press the door of the shipping container with my palms and slide it shut behind me, wanting to be in this space alone, undisturbed, so I can look for an answer to where Cory might have taken my little girl.

After I have touched several surfaces, it dawns on me that this is a crime scene. I know I am out of my depth here, but I don't want to leave now. Not yet. Trying to be more careful of the fact it is a crime scene, I begin walking around the container with open eyes. Not the kind of eyes I had when I lived at Garden Temple, when I pretended the things I saw were not reality, pretended that I wasn't in a prison of my own making.

I'm not a woman who pretends anymore. Now I am a woman who is strong, who knows what she wants, a mother who is desperate for her child and will do anything it takes to keep her safe.

The day has been so long. I'm still stunned that Jeremiah was here in my home, his eyes on mine. My skin crawls at the memory of all those times he did more than look at me with his eyes, the times he razed his hands over my skin, pinned me to my bed, had his way with me.

I squeeze my eyes shut, not wanting to think about the worst, about the horrible things that could be happening to my little girl right now.

It makes me nauseous, ill, to consider my little girl being violated in any way.

I thought I was done crying, but it's not tears of sorrow that are building up in my chest now—it's tears of terror. Cory's container is a pitiful place, a stained mattress on the ground that must have been dragged here from some bedroom at his grandma's house, an armchair that is threadbare and pale blue. Empty beer cans and wrappers from hamburgers litter the floor. LED lights circle the place, and I stand on my tiptoes clicking them on. A dizzying neon light show envelops me, blinking wildly as if to mock me.

Was Ruthie here? Did she see these lights? Did she lie on this bed? There are random books on the floor, none I recognize, some old manga comics and notepads with the scrawling hand of a teenage boy across them. I notice a guitar propped in the corner missing a string. Not much to go on. There's an ashtray with cigarette butts and a bong half filled with murky water on a table. I pick up a notepad knowing I probably shouldn't, but shouldn'ts were forgotten the moment I left my house and said I was looking for fresh air when I was really looking for answers. Looking for some sort of truth.

I sink into the blue armchair, surprised that it holds my weight, it's so rickety. I pick up a spiral notebook on the floor, noticing the front page is filled with lyrics, maybe a poem.

I'm looking for answers / I'm looking for hope

Looking for a way out / a way to cope.

I know that it's wrong / but I'm done being right.

I can't wait til the morning / I'll go tonight.

I reread the lines. The rest of the notebook is empty, and I find my fingers tracing his sloppy writing, wondering if the boy who wrote this knows where my little girl is, if the boy who wrote this has left her alone somewhere.

The longer he refuses to tell the truth to Boone and the rest of the officers at the police department, the longer Ruthie will be alone. I reread the poem a dozen times. Being in this container should creep me out, but the idea that Ruthie was here somehow comforts me. Makes me feel closer to her. I pray she is nearby. That I will have her in my arms tomorrow. I can't bear another night without her.

Eventually, my eyelids fall closed. Though I blink to keep them open and the ridiculous lights blasting around me should keep me awake, it's impossible. *I can't wait for the morning / I'll go tonight.*

I jerk awake, sitting up in the blue chair. Looking around, the neon lights mocking me, the notebook still in my hand, I look at my watch. It's 5:00 a.m. That is a long walk for fresh air.

I rub my hands over my eyes, angry at myself for falling asleep for so long, my body lulled into slumber by this teenage boy's words. My stomach rumbles; my body aches as if I've been in a fistfight and a throw-down when, in fact, I haven't raised my fists at all. I raised my voice, I suppose, my heart rate too. Still, my whole body feels weary and weak, exhaustion covering me.

I stand, knowing I need to get back to my house, assuming everyone is worried now that they've realized I've been gone for so long. MacArthur will be pissed. It was his job to make sure I was okay. I'll explain it all to them once I get there. It's not his fault I couldn't stay still.

I stand, walking to the switch for the LED lights, flipping them off. As I do, my eyes land on a piece of paper on the floor, not one with Cory's scrawled handwriting, but a very distinct kind of paper, a paper crane folded intricately. I pick it up, holding it in my hand, thinking of Ruthie's crane resting on her dresser. Her obsession with origami the last few weeks.

My fingers wrap around the origami crane. I slide it into my pocket, needing to get home. I need to talk to the police. I know Cory took my daughter.

24

It's still dark as I step out of Cory's bunker. The crisp morning air promising a day that is dry. I hope so; clear skies will help with our search. I close the door of the shipping container and run, desperate to get home. I stumble over my feet. My chest pounds, but I need to find Boone, to speak to someone who will listen, because this paper crane means something. The piece of paper in my pocket means Cory Jacobson has her—he must. If the coat wasn't enough, and the barrette wasn't enough, maybe this crane will be.

When I get to my street, I see cops everywhere, and I instantly know that they are looking for me. But then another thought crosses my mind. Maybe it's not about me at all. Maybe they found Ruthie.

I pull my phone from my pocket, wondering if maybe I missed calls, but it's dead. The battery died long ago. I curse myself for being so stupid, for sleeping for so long. As I get up to the house, people seem to notice that I'm running toward them.

"Gray?" Truce says. "Damn, where have you been? We've been worried sick."

"I know," I say. "I fell asleep, and my phone died ..." I run my hands over my eyes. "Do you know where Boone is?" I ask. "I need to talk to him."

"Yeah, he's down at the mobile command unit. Want me to radio him over right now?"

"Yes, please," I say. "Did I miss anything?" I ask after he finishes radioing Boone. "Something with Ruthie? With Cory, did you guys find anything out? God, I can't believe I slept for so long."

Olive and Abel walk toward me from the house, bundled up in their coats.

"Mom, where'd you go?" Olive asks. "We've been so worried."

"MacArthur's pissed," Abel adds.

"I know. I'm sorry. I fell asleep. I'm really,

really sorry. I didn't mean to. I know I'm terrible, but ..."

"Hey, it's okay," Truce says. "You're okay. You're here. You're okay. Your body shut down because you needed to rest. We all get it. Charlie is on her way back now too." Truce repeats, "It's okay."

I'm amazed at his ability—the ability of all the police officers—to help me release the foothold of panic that's wound around my chest.

"Okay," I say, taking a big, deep breath. "You're right. We're okay. I'm okay. Olive, Abel, are you guys okay?"

"We're okay, Mom," Olive says. She wraps me in her arms, giving me a big tight hug, and I breathe her in. Thankful for her, for this girl of mine to be here holding me steady.

"You guys get some good rest?" I ask them both, and they nod.

"They still haven't found her," Abel says, walking in a circle.

"I know, but I think I can help. I know it's got to be Cory," I say just as Boone jogs down the sidewalk. The streetlamp outside my house casts a glow across him.

"Let's go inside," I tell everyone. "It's freezing out here."

Inside, Boone asks where I went. I lick my lips. "You're not going to like this," I tell him, "but I went to Cory's shipping container."

Boone's eyes narrow. "You did what?" He groans with frustration. "Gray, what were you thinking?"

"I was thinking that I need to find my daughter is what I was thinking," I say, raising my voice. "I'm thinking I can't sit around here and just wait. The clock is ticking, Boone. I was there at the police station. I heard what he was saying, and it was going nowhere. I needed to see if I could find an answer or a reason or something."

Boone shakes his head. "Gray, it wasn't Cory."

"What do you mean, it wasn't Cory? I know it was him," I insist, thinking of the crane in my pocket.

"No," Boone says, addressing me gently. "It really wasn't. I came here about to talk to you in case you were up. We finally got a confession out of the kid."

"Okay, and what did he confess? Does he know where she is?"

"No," Boone says, "he doesn't. His confession had to do with his alibi and it checks out."

"He said he was at the shipping container, the shipping container I was at, and he didn't know and ..."

"Gray," Boone says, his voice firm and direct, "you need to sit down and listen, okay? I know this is hard to hear. I know you wanted an answer, and if saying it was Cory might get you closer to your daughter, I understand why you would want us to follow that lead, but I'm telling you, the kid had nothing to do with Ruthie's kidnapping."

"So who did?" I ask. "Who did?"

"What's his alibi?" Abel asks.

"The reason he was so hesitant to tell us the truth was because of those two priors. He knew if he had a third, it could lock him up. And he was scared because he knew his alibi would land him behind bars."

I frown. "But it doesn't have to do with Ruthie?"

Boone shakes his head. "No, Gray, it doesn't. He's been selling drugs out of that container. Pot to minors, pills. He steals from his grandma mostly and buys from other guys in the neighborhood." He runs the back of his palm through his hair. "I know it's not what you wanted to hear, but it's the truth. We were able to question the guys he ratted out, the ones who he was selling to at the time that Ruthie was taken, and it adds up."

"Maybe they're just protecting him," I say. "Maybe these guys who bought from him on that night were just trying to cover for him. How can you be sure?"

"Because it all makes sense. Cory broke down crying, admitting why he was scared to explain what he was doing, why his alibi was so shaky. His grandma also acknowledged that she's been having all of her pills stolen and that she's been having a real heck of a time with her doctors and the pharmacy. And she knew it was Cory, but also knew the consequence of saying anything, that her grandson would be behind bars."

"Is he?" Abel asks. "Is he staying in jail because of this?"

"He'll have an arraignment, and a judge will decide, but it doesn't look good, especially in light of the situation. Cory was withholding his alibi to protect himself, and in doing so, we spent precious hours going down a road that was a dead end, hours that could mean life or death for your sister," Boone says plainly. "So in my estimation, Cory screwed himself in his decision." He looks at Olive and Abel closely. "Which is a good lesson to remind everyone that it's very important to tell the truth even if it gets you in trouble. Cory learned that the hard way this week."

"So it's not Cory," I say in disbelief. I'd been so sure. "And if it's not Cory ..." I swallow, not wanting to cry again. Those blasted tears keep surfacing, and even when I think I'm all dried up, I'm not. Maybe a mother never is. Maybe a mother who loses a child could still cry at the drop of the hat for the love lost a decade later, two, more.

Charlie Callahan walks into my house just then and comes over, kneeling beside me, her hand on my back.

"Hey," she says, "how you doing?"

"I've been better, a whole lot better," I say. "It's not Cory and it's not Jeremiah and it's not Jasper. And so, who is it that has my little girl? Who is it? Who would do this to me, do this to us?"

Boone drops his hands in defeat, and I know he feels to blame for not having an answer, but he's not to blame because he didn't take my little girl.

But someone, someone did.

And I can't stop until I know who.

I can't stop until I have my little girl back in my arms.

25

MAYBE IT'S because I'm practically hysterical, but Charlie tells me I need to go upstairs, take a shower, and put on some clean clothes. I don't think it's because I smell. I think it's because a steaming hot shower might clear my head or at least give me a place to cry privately.

Someone's at the door, and Charlie answers it just as I'm rounding the corner to go upstairs. My neighbor Julia is handing over freshly baked quiche and a box of donuts.

"The least I can do," she says, giving me a quick wave.

"Thank you," I tell her, my voice hoarse, before turning and heading up the stairs. I'm not in a place to tell her that we have no leads, no answers.

In my bedroom, I look through my drawers for some comfortable clothes and pull out jeans, a T-shirt, and a sweater. I charge my phone on my bedside table, and then walk across the hall to the bathroom, locking the door behind me.

I turn on the water, feeling like I just did this yesterday. Feeling like my whole world is on a terrible cycle of heartbreak. I brush my teeth before stepping into the hot shower. I let the scorching water run over my skin as I close my eyes, telling myself that this isn't the end, that Ruthie is still out there, that we will fight to find her.

I think of the words of Cory's poem. Last night I thought that they were true, that ending things tonight meant him taking my little girl. When in reality, they must've meant something else altogether.

Maybe Cory was planning on hurting himself, doing something irreversible. Now he won't have that opportunity if he's behind bars.

I like to think the world will be a safer place if there isn't a teenager dealing drugs on the train tracks. But I don't know if it's as simple as that. Because the dangerous people aren't always the obvious ones. Jeremiah isn't. He's charming and polite. He can work a room, and certainly work a woman. Yet he's more dangerous than anyone I've ever met.

Maybe it's the same for the person who took my little girl. Maybe it's a wolf in sheep's clothing.

I wash my hair. I scrub my skin. I step out of the shower and dress in the bathroom, not wanting to cross the hall in a towel with so many people coming and going from my house. In my bedroom I run a comb through my hair and I check my phone.

Now that it's turned back on, there are lots of text messages that I was not mentally able to answer yesterday. But now I sit on the edge of my bed and type out responses to the group chat with my neighbors and texts from my coworkers at the library. Everyone showing signs of support and words of encouragement, letting me know they are prepared to go back out and search today.

I reply with *thank you* and *I appreciate it*, and *let's not give up hope*. I tell them how much it means to me, how the food has been a godsend, how their relentless care and concern for me and my family is an act of love that has not gone unnoticed.

The sun is rising now, and when I stand to look out my window, I see the news vans are still here, and it gives me a sense of hope.

It's a new day. My little girl has been missing for forty hours, but it does not mean that she is gone forever.

I slip my phone in my back jeans pocket, putting on my sneakers, lacing them. I pause at Olive's bedroom door. Her bed is made, a stuffed animal in the center of her pillow. Tidiness and cleanliness went hand in hand back at Garden Temple, and her room is a testament to that early childhood rearing.

The next door down is Ruthie's. I pull it open and step inside, wanting to be close to her in ways I can't be until she's back in this bed and under this roof. With a prayer of hope in my heart, I stand at the mirror above her dresser and finger through all her pretty barrettes, her sparkly hair clips, the glittering trinkets of an eight-year-old.

I pluck out a faux diamond-encrusted barrette, and I clip it in my hair. Not caring if I look ridiculous. Desperate to be closer to her. Among her things is the paper crane, and I pick it up, considering it again. This one here, and one in Cory's bunker. They're strange, these cranes.

I walk downstairs, smelling coffee brewing again, and hear Abel and Olive watching something on my laptop computer. When they see me, Olive closes it immediately as if she's been caught.

"It's okay," I say softly. "I know it's impossible to just stand around and cry for days on end. It's okay to smile and laugh. Okay? Don't feel guilty about that," I tell her. She nods but doesn't open the computer again. Abel asks if I want coffee and I say yes. He knows I will never say no.

Next to the computer, Olive has a slice of quiche and orange juice, and some paper and markers.

With coffee in hand, I notice Charlie is in the living room typing on her tablet. Besides that, though, the house is empty. Quiet. I admit to feeling a bit of relief in that, knowing everyone in the Tacoma Police Department has seen me at my very worst at this point. I'm not exactly thrilled at the idea of them seeing that in real time for another day. I also wonder just how long a police department works on finding a missing child. How long before they quit, before they stop altogether, driving the mobile command unit back to the police station, before the news crews leave, before the stories stop being reported, before Ruthie goes missing forever?

I sit down at the kitchen table with my coffee, look over at Olive. She has a lined piece of notebook paper, and she folds it at one angle, then another. The creases precise.

"What are you doing?" I ask.

She shrugs. "Origami."

"Yeah," I say. "You and your sister are really into that, huh?"

She smiles. "I guess. I don't know. Granger always gives us paper cranes."

"Granger? Our neighbor?"

She nods. "Yeah."

"The guy down the street?"

"I guess he moved in like a month ago."

"When do you see him?" I ask, remembering his shy smile at the circulation desk a few days ago. I'd wondered if he was flirting with me. In fact, I'm sure he was.

"I don't know. He's usually out by the bus. His house is right in front of the stop."

"I take you to the bus stop in the morning."

"No, I mean in the afternoon," she says, not looking up. She's finished the crane and slides it over to me. "Do you know how to make origami?"

"No," I say. "I've never tried in my life."

"You should have looked at that how-to book we got last week at the library."

All at once my whole body tenses, tight.

The coffee falls from my hand, pouring all over the table, dripping to the floor.

"Mom, what is it?" Olive asks.

Abel rushes to the kitchen and grabs a towel. "Mom. Are you okay?"

"No," I say, shaking my head. "Charlie, come here."

"What is it, Gray?" she asks. "What's going on?"

"I know who has Ruthie," I say. "I know who has my little girl."

26

Boone is radioed to my home, along with some other officers from the police department. And quickly, my home becomes the new mobile command unit as I sit at my kitchen table explaining to them what I've already said to Charlie.

"It's Granger," I repeat, "my neighbor down the street."

"The one who has been leading the search parties?" Truce asks, frowning.

I nod. "Yes, it's him. He came into the library the other day and checked out a stack of books, which he does often. He started coming into the library really frequently. And one of the books was on origami. And Olive says he gives paper cranes to the kids after school."

Olive shakes her head. "No, Mom, not the kids. Just Ruthie and me."

I pause at her words, the weight of them. Granger has been watching Ruthie. Making a plan. My stomach seizes with fear. "Okay," I say, needing to remain collected to get through my statement. "So he gives paper cranes to Ruthie and Olive. And they've got them in their bedrooms, and I found one in Cory's shipping container."

Charlie lifts her eyebrows. "You went to his shipping container?" Somehow she missed that briefing.

"Yes," I say, knowing it wasn't the smartest thing. But now that it has led me here, I'm glad I followed my intuition. "Last night I left the house and went on a walk. I went there on purpose. I was just so determined to find an answer. I was sick of being at dead ends. And I was going crazy in the house, so I went. And I found this," I say, walking to my coat that hangs on a hook by the door, pulling out the crumpled paper crane. "This was in his shipping container."

"The same place we found her coat, correct?" Truce asks.

"Yes, exactly. Granger must have planted it there," I explain. "Believe me."

Boone listens closely, not dismissing my opinion. The other officers must take my words seriously, too, because within minutes, all the police officers are congregating on my street, making a plan.

I won't be left in the shadows though. If Granger has my little girl, I am going to find her.

With my coat on, I follow the police officers as they march toward Granger's house.

Truce turns to me. "You can't be here, Gray."

I shake my head. "Like hell I can't. What are they going to do, handcuff me? Put me in a police car? Lock me inside my house? No. If my little girl is with Granger, I want to know. I want to see her. I want to hold her."

When we get to Granger's house, Boone takes the lead. "Has the current search party Granger is leading already left?"

An officer lifts a hand in the air. "We just radioed for them to return. They're on their way."

"Maybe she's in his house," I suggest. "Can't we just go in?"

"No," Boone says, "we can't just go in. And Gray, you really shouldn't be here."

"Yes, I should." I say, standing my ground as I see a group from the neighborhood moving toward the commotion in front of Granger's house. Everyone is watching, scared, concerned. *What are they all doing here? What has Granger got to do with anything? It's a lot of officers all in one place.* Whispers and worries, and I can relate because I'm worried too. Terrified, actually.

"Boone, you need to see this," Charlie says, handing him her tablet. A few minutes pass, Boone and Charlie both reading the tablet in Boone's hands, processing information. But I can't hear what they are saying from where I am standing. I step toward them, frustrated, but that is when a dozen police mobilize in front of me, and it's obvious they have a plan in place.

Shortly, Granger, along with a group of people, rounds the corner and heads up to his front yard.

"What's going on?" he asks, hands on his hips. "Can I help? They just radioed us to come back in."

"Do you have her?" I ask, stepping

forward, knowing I am completely out of line.

"Gray, enough," Boone says, but I shake him off.

"Do you have her?" I shout.

Granger looks at me, worried. "Gray, what are you talking about?"

"Do you have Ruthie? Did you take her? Where did you take her?"

Granger's eyes crease with concern. "I didn't take her anywhere. I swear to you, Gray." He chuckles. "Gray, I'm just here helping. Just doing my part as a neighbor."

Boone, though, clears his throat. "Just like you did your part eighteen months ago, down in Olympia, Washington?" he asks slowly. I turn, looking to Boone, not understanding what this is about. "You were connected to a kidnapping case there too, weren't you?"

He frowns. "Connected? It wasn't like that."

"Then why don't you explain what it was like?" Boone presses.

"I suppose it was a case of being in the right place at the right time."

"Was it though?" Boone asks, his words chosen with care. "Because my colleague just gave me some incredibly damaging reports about you, Granger. And you were the one who found the missing child. The missing child of a single mother who fits the profile of Gray. Same hair, same eyes, same body type."

Granger backs away. "No, no. I just, I lived in Olympia, that's where I worked. And there was a girl that got abducted, and we formed a search party. A lot like this. And—"

"And you just happened to find a little girl, and reunite her with her mother?"

"Yes," Granger says. But his eyes twitch, and he wrings his hands together. And I realize if he was flirting with me at the library, it was because he wanted to get close to me. "Saving" my daughter would ensure my loyalty laid with him.

"Where is she?" I ask.

"I don't know," Granger says. "I swear. I swear. I just—"

"You just were preparing yourself to mysteriously discover where Ruthie was, and reunite her with her mother?" Boone asks without a trace of emotion in his voice. "We need to search your home."

"You can't go in there!" Granger says, his voice raised. "It's my private property!"

"We're bypassing a search warrant, and we're going in," Boone tells his officers.

"Granger needs to be detained while we search."

"This is ridiculous!" Granger shouts. "I'm a good guy. I swear!"

"I thought everyone on the street was interviewed already," I say to York, who stands beside me.

"They were," York tells me. "But we don't just go into every single person's home and scour it. Not without probable cause."

"And now?" I say. "You have cause? Boone," I shout, walking closer to him. "Why didn't you say something about Granger's past before?"

"I just figured it out," he said. "I ran a search on the name after you voiced your worry, and it came up in the database. Thankfully, he stayed in Washington State."

"You really think Ruthie might be in there?" I say as they walk toward the front door.

He swallows. "I sure as hell hope so."

My heart pounds as they open the door to Granger's home, and I watch as five officers enter his residence. My hands are pressed together as I watch, wait.

"I want to go in," I tell Charlie. "Can't I please go in?"

"No," she says. "You can't; you really can't. Just wait, Gray. We don't know what's in there. We don't know what we might find."

Tears spill down my cheeks. "But she's my baby."

"I know," she says, reaching for my hand and squeezing it.

I turn to Charlie. "I'm so scared," I say. This woman I've just met has become my confidant, my therapist, my real-world version of a sister wife. She has my back, and I make a vow in this moment that when we come out of this, on the other side, I'll have her back too. Whatever she needs, I'll be there for her. Because in my darkest hour, she's been at my side.

And she stands by me now, assuming I'll wait.

But I'm tired of waiting. Pacing. Hoping.

I run toward the house, bypassing the officers. Not caring that they call after me to stop. I climb the steps of Granger's freshly painted porch, pushing inside, taking in the room. He's got a big TV, a few recliners. It's clean and quiet. But I know my daughter is here. On his coffee table there are the library books I checked out to him.

My eyes dart from one place to the next, needing to see Ruthie.

"Where is she?" I cry, pushing away the officers standing at the basement door, ready to open it.

I move Boone away, forcing him back, my fingers on the locks. One. Two. Three. I flip them open as Boone tells me to step aside.

"I can't," I shout at him. "I won't. I need to find her!"

With the locks open, I pull back the unassuming steel door and run downstairs into the basement.

This is the part that should be the scariest, walking into the dark nether regions of the house, where my little girl is held captive.

But when I get downstairs, I find a fully insulated rec room. There's another big TV, a stack of DVDs, also from the library. Books too. Origami paper and cranes scattered everywhere.

A nondescript room that I know Ruthie would never be able to identify. If Granger took her down here blindfolded, she'd never know who her captor was. There's a mini fridge, and empty juice boxes, a jar of peanut butter and jelly, a loaf of white bread. There are potato chip bags, and a bowl of fruit, and a bathroom even. But no windows.

I take in all of these details in a moment. In an instant. One second is all it takes before my eyes land on my daughter standing in the corner, eyes wide, trembling.

She runs to me. Ruthie wraps her arms around my waist, and I hold her tight. Breathing her in. She is in one piece and whole and here. "Oh, Ruthie," I gasp. "I got you, sweetheart. I won't let you go."

"Mama," she sobs. "Oh Mama, I missed you."

27

I CAN'T LET GO of Ruthie. I won't, not after what she's just been through. I lift her up in my arms, and even though she's not a toddler, she's still only eight, small enough to hold. Her legs wrap around my waist, and she clings to my neck, and I kiss her cheeks over and over and over again.

"Mama's here," I whisper, my tears on her cheeks, her heart my heart. My love for her overflowing. She wraps her arms around my neck, refusing to let go.

We climb the steps. Boone's hand is on the small of my back as I climb them, making sure I don't fall back, but nothing happens to Ruthie or me.

As we pass through the basement door, a

chill runs over me. The locks on the door kept her in. I want the whole house to burn to the ground. There's no way Ruthie could've gotten out, no way she could have escaped. I want to know if she tried, what she thought, if Granger went down there at all. But I'm sure he didn't. I'm sure he brought her here, made sure she had no idea who it was who carried her down the steps into that room and then left her there for forty hours to fend for herself.

At eight, she was old enough to feed herself and use the bathroom. She would have been scared, of course, but she eventually would have watched TV and fallen asleep on the couch with a blanket wrapped around her. She must've been terrified.

I want to ask about all of these things, but I know I can't. Not now, not when she's so fragile, shaking in my arms, terrified. If Granger had been the one to find her, blindfolded, and miraculously deliver her unscathed to me, claiming he found her in some abandoned house, maybe the police would have believed him. From Boone's statements, it's clear they believed him before.

As I walk out of Granger's house, I

consider how easy it is to believe someone, to trust their good intentions. How is someone supposed to discern good from evil, right from wrong? I want to go with my gut, but I feel like I have a lot to learn when it comes to intuition. It's like my DNA has me dead set on trusting the wrong people. Jeremiah and Patrick and Granger, I'm lining up these men, and none of them intended to do me good. They all intended to do me harm.

"Mommy," Ruthie says in my ear, "I don't like to be alone."

"I know, baby. I know."

We exit Granger's house, and my entire neighborhood is here. There are news cameras everywhere filming the entire thing. Reporters with microphones documenting each moment, each step I take, zooming in on the little girl in my arms. There's no blood, no broken bones. She has not been hurt externally. Internally, that's another question. Childhood trauma is real. I've read about it over the last year, checking out books on child development from the library, learning about adverse childhood experiences, about brain development. My only hope is that I've loved my little girl long enough and hard enough that she knows that in an unsafe world, she is still safe because she has me.

The roar from the crowd is wild, fierce, full of elation, and I find myself smiling, shaking, crying, everything at once because my little girl is here. Olive and Abel rush across the wet and muddy grass. Piles of snow are still accumulated, not yet melted, and they crunch over them as they pull Ruthie and me into their arms, the four of us together. Together. I won't let go. I won't lose them, never, never.

"Ruthie," Olive sobs, "I missed you."

"I missed you too, sis," Ruthie says, climbing down from my arms and wrapping her sister in the biggest hug. Tears are flying down their cheeks, but I know what kind of tears they are, made from relief and the purest love.

Abel is breaking down, his shoulders shaking with a release I understand. "Oh, Mom," he says, "you didn't give up."

"I never will," I say. "I will never give up fighting for my children."

Everyone is so happy, the kind of pure joy that is rare, that you see maybe at weddings when everyone is delighted and hopeful, believing in the promise of love.

That's what I feel right now. It's a feeling I want to hold on to for a long, long time. Forever.

Later, after we've given our reports to the officers, after Granger has left handcuffed, cursed by everyone who witnessed the recovery of my little girl, I give Ruthie a bath.

I wash her hair, lather her long blonde curls. "Did you try and find me?" she asks. "The whole time?"

"We didn't stop looking," I promise her. "We never would. You are our treasure, Ruthie."

After she's dressed in cozy clothing, I comb her hair, sitting on the edge of her bed. She sits crossed-legged on the floor, smelling of lavender and bubble bath.

"Can I have the pretty barrettes?" she asks.

"Of course," I say, wanting her to have pretty barrettes everyday of her life from here on forward, as I am reminded of her lost things scattered in Cory's yard and in his shipping container.

We've learned by now that Granger planted them, wanting to point fingers at someone else.

Now I clip purple flower hair clips in

Ruthie's hair, done into double French braids with ribbons tied at the ends.

"Perfect," I say, and she stands, giving me another hug. I hear music downstairs, coming from a piano, and I take Ruthie's hands, refusing to let go of her. In the living room, Olive sits with her back straight on the piano bench, her fingers trailing over the keys, playing a melody I know, a hymn we've sung a thousand times. *It is well. It is well in my soul.*

Luna is here with Sophie and her husband, Bart, and a few men I don't know are leaving the house with a dolly.

"I know you need time as a family," Luna says. "But I just thought music makes everything a little bit better, and your little girl, Olive, is so good on the piano. I thought she could put better use to our old piano than I can."

"Thank you, Luna," Olive says politely. "It's such a generous gift."

Luna bats her away. "Honey, you deserve all the happiness in the world." Luna's eyes are filled with tears, and God, this neighborhood has been crying more this week than I think we ever have in our lives. But I guess that's what happens when you're confronted with the reality that life is so precious, that our children are a gift to never take for granted.

Sophie walks over to Ruthie and gives her a big hug. "I'm so happy you're home," she says.

Ruthie smiles up at her. "Me too. I was scared we would never get that sleepover you promised me."

Sophie winks. "I promise, it will happen as soon as your mom gives us the okay."

Luna gives me a hug, squeezing me tight. "Oh honey, we're here for you. You understand?"

I nod, believing her. After her family leaves, it's just Charlie and Boone who are left. Charlie's packing up her messenger bag, the tablet she's carried nonstop slipped inside.

She surprises me when she pulls out her phone. "I know this is probably not the most professional thing, but now that this case is closed, can I have your number? I know right now you have a lot going on, but I thought maybe eventually when things settle, we could get coffee? As friends?"

"Yes," I say, taking it from her and

entering my contact information. "I would love to get together."

"Good," Charlie says. "I would too." She kneels down in front of my daughter. "Ruthie, you are a very special girl, and I am so glad to see you safe back at home with your mom and your brother and sister. They all love you so very much."

Ruthie smiles shyly. "Thanks, Charlie." Her voice is soft and timid. And I exhale, her voice music to my ears.

Charlie leaves, making eye contact with Boone, maybe warning him to not do something stupid. Charlie understands that Boone being on this case wouldn't have happened in the future. Because in the future, the friendship I have with him may skirt the line of acceptable. Maybe it already does.

She leaves, and Boone clears his throat. "Well, I don't want to overstay my welcome." I know he's so worried for us, all of us.

I shake my head. "It's okay," I say. "There's plenty of food and ..."

Boone nods. "I know, but you guys have had a hell of a weekend."

Olive shakes her head. "Let me just warm up some food, and we can eat together before you go," she offers, and I have a feeling that Boone's presence here comforts her the same way it comforts me.

"Thanks, Olive, but I gotta go home to my dog, Matisse. He's been with the neighbor for a few days, and I need to take him off her hands. A rain check though?"

Olive smiles. "Okay, a rain check."

I walk Boone to the front door, the kids heading to the kitchen to get some food ready.

"Thank you," I say as he pulls on his winter coat. "For everything."

His eyes level with mine. "You're a good mom," he tells me. "And a hell of an investigator. You ever think of being a police officer?"

I smile wryly. "Never, actually."

"Right, you always dreamed of being a florist, right?"

"You remembered that?"

His eyebrows lift. "I remember."

I swallow, not knowing what Boone is to me beyond a friend who makes me feel seen and heard, who believes in my strength. Who believes in me.

"I know last time we said goodbye, I told you I'd call when I was ready ..."

Boone runs a hand over his jaw. "You did call; it just wasn't for a date."

"You wanted a date?"

He smirks. "I know I'm rusty, but I thought you knew that."

"I've never been asked out before, is all."

Boone reaches toward me, his calloused hand on my cheek. "I want a date, Gray."

"Me too," I whisper.

"Dinner's ready," Olive shouts, and I step back.

"I will call you," I tell him. "Under happier circumstances next time. I promise."

He leaves, and I stand in the doorway, watching him leave. He gives me a final wave before getting in his car, and I walk away, not sure where this is going but trusting that in time I will know.

SOON THE FOUR of us are sitting at a table with piping hot homemade macaroni and cheese and soda, a rare treat for my children. Right now I will give them literally anything they ask for. Olive is gushing over the cheesy pasta, and Ruthie is grinning at everything

Abel says, finding comfort in her big brother's presence.

Abel pulls out his phone, frowning. "I missed a call."

I immediately think of Bethany, of Garden Temple, of how our work is not yet done. We may be sitting here eating in peace right now, but this will not last. Soon, very soon, we need to get to Eastern Washington and help Bethany escape.

She's carrying my son's child. And if she is discovered to have lain with a man besides her future husband before her wedding, it's going to be bad.

He tries to call the number back, but there is no answer.

"Did she leave a message?" I ask.

He shakes his head, biting his bottom lip. "No."

We finish eating, and by the time we wash up the dishes, we're all yawning, exhaustion from the last two days finally catching up to us.

Tucking Ruthie into bed is long and drawn out, and she doesn't want me to finish the chapter book I'm reading aloud. "Can I sleep with you?" she asks.

"Of course, baby, I'm gonna check on your

brother and sister, but I'll be right back, okay?"

I let Olive and Abel stay up to watch a movie, thinking they would most likely fall asleep on the couch, but feeling like that scenario is the most normal thing they could do. The sort of normal thing I have always wanted for them.

"I love you both, so much," I tell them before triple checking the locks on both the front and back doors. I know Granger is locked up, but I don't feel the same sense of safety I felt a week ago. I hope one day it returns. For now, I will wrap my children up with mother's love and pray it protects them.

In the morning I wake rested in a way I haven't in ages. Ruthie is hot and sweaty beside me, and I gasp when I open my eyes and see someone standing over my bed.

"Olive?" I sit up. "What is it?"

She's shaking.

"Sorry, Mom, I should have said something earlier ... I just ... I just didn't know what to do. I promised ..."

"Promised what, sweetie?" I take her

cheeks between my hands. "What is happening? Where's your brother?"

"That's the thing," she whimpers. "Abel left. He told me not to say anything, but ..."

"You're doing the right thing. Was he going to Bethany?"

Olive nods. "I took his phone from his backpack when he wasn't looking. He was going to catch a bus."

"When?"

"Last night, after you went to bed."

My heart falls. Why didn't Olive tell me sooner?

I can't say that aloud though, because her eyes are rimmed in red, and she's clearly upset over her decision.

"I listened to his phone messages this morning," she says, crying now. "I wanted to know why he had to leave so fast. And he lied, Mom. Last night he said Bethany didn't leave a message, but she did."

"Where is the phone?" I ask. Ruthie stirs beside me, rubbing her eyes.

"What's happening?" Ruthie asks.

"Shh, sweetie. Shh, it's okay," I soothe, knowing my words are absolute lies. Nothing is okay.

Olive hands me the small, black flip

phone, and I press the button for messages, finding the one from last night. Putting it on speaker, I turn up the volume.

"Abel, I know you're still looking for Ruthie," Bethany says. "But I really hope you can make it back to Garden Temple soon. The prophet has told us his revelation. We've been waiting for so many years for this time, for this moment, and it's here. Our garden has grown and it's time to return. It's time for all of us to return to Eden."

The message ends and my heart drops. Jeremiah left one day ago, angry at me, at the children. Humiliated by our rejection.

Is this his way of getting payback? Has he realized his reign is over?

I cover my mouth. "Oh God."

"What does it mean, Mom?" Olive asks, her eyes wide, not understanding. And for that, I am grateful. It's my job to protect her. "Where did they go? Where is Eden?"

I try to still my shaking hands, fearing the worst. If they've gone to Eden, they'll never be coming back.

Preorder Book Two Now: The Sister Wife's Husband

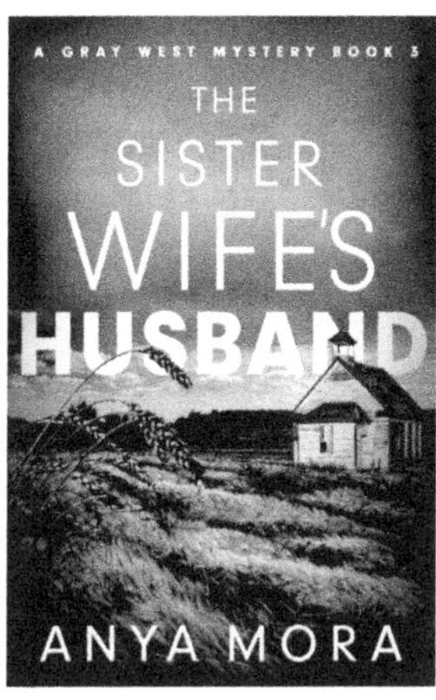

My husband has always been dangerous.
But I never thought he was a killer.
One phone message changes everything.
The cult where I spent fifteen years of my life is preparing for the unthinkable.
My son has returned to the fold.
I must find him before it is too late.
But it's not just his life that's at stake – it's the entire congregation of Garden Temple.
I thought I was destined to be a sister-wife and mother, but turns out, I am so much more.
I am a woman who must stop my husband's

madness before he does something
irreversible.
I must stop him before it's too late.

This is book three in a new suspense series.
Preorder Now: On Amazon

ALSO BY:

THE WIFE LIE

My husband is missing.
And his wife is on my doorstep.
The wife I never knew he had.

Does that mean my husband's out looking for wife number three?
The more I dig... the more I find.
Ledger Stone is not the man I thought I knew.
What I'd thought was a whirlwind romance has turned out to be a hurricane laced with lies.
It started with one.
Will it end with another?

The Wife Lie is a domestic suspense novel where secrets are buried deep.
Penny Stone gave up everything for the husband she thought she knew -- and now she must uncover the truth: just how much of her marriage was a lie?
And is their love worth fighting for?

DOWNLOAD NOW: On Amazon

TUESDAY'S CHILD

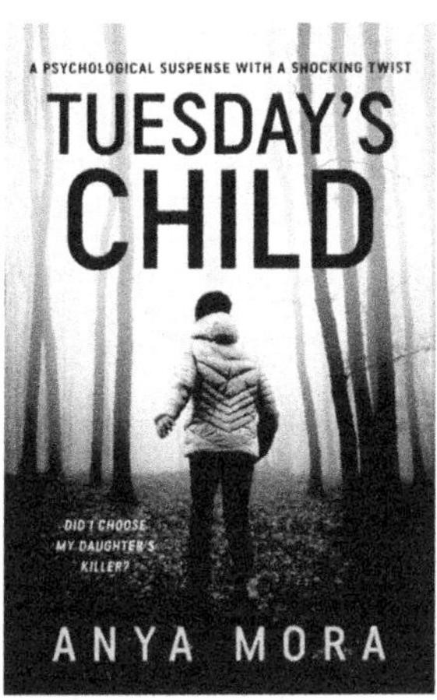

My daughter is dead.
My husband and I cling to what's left of our family, desperate to make sense of the tragedy.
But when the sheriff knocks, he delivers news no mother should ever have to hear.
Our daughter was murdered.
And my son is the prime suspect.

When we adopted eleven-year-old Holden, we weren't wearing rose-colored glasses.
But we never could have imagined this.

They say you can't pick your family.
But I picked mine.
Did I choose my daughter's murderer?

Tuesday's Child is a gripping domestic suspense. Doubt, desire, and the demise of a once picture-perfect family force Emery, wife to a state senator, to live out a mother's worst nightmare.

DOWNLOAD NOW: On Amazon

SECRETS MOTHERS KEEP

On Friday night in the clay fields of Bethel Creek, seventeen-year-old Daniel Reyes is found brutally attacked and left for dead. On Saturday morning, Cora Maxwell finds her teenage son's clothes covered in blood. A small town torn apart by a horrific hate crime.

An investigative reporter hell bent on finding the truth.
A mother's worst nightmare.
What really happened to the Reyes boy?

In the heart-stopping and timely suspense novel, Secrets Mothers Keep, widow and mother Cora Maxwell faces the hardest decision of her life.
In a world where there are few second chances, do you grant one to your child?
And if so... what is the cost?

DOWNLOAD NOW: On Amazon

ABOUT THE AUTHOR

Anya Mora lives in the Pacific Northwest with her family. Her novels, while leaning toward the dark, ultimately reflect light, courage, and her innate belief that love rewards the brave.

To learn about sales and new releases, sign up for Mora's mailing list here: https://anyamora.com/newsletter/

Made in the USA
Las Vegas, NV
20 September 2021

30697728R00164